A nine-year-old girl is sent to a country farm to serve her probation for shoplifting – a characteristic Icelandic sentence. In this powerful, unchanging landscape she finds a community torn between ancient tradition and new attitudes. This is no bucolic idyll: she must confront new and painful feelings and has to face the unknown within herself and in her alien surroundings. Gradually, by submitting to the inevitable restraints and suffering of remote rural life, she finds a kind of freedom.

SHAD THAMES BOOKS

Also in this series:

For details of Mare's Nest books, please see pages 145–52.

The Swan

Published in 1997
in the Shad Thames series
by Mare's Nest Publishing
49 Norland Square London W11 4PZ

The Swan
Gudbergur Bergsson

Copyright © Gudbergur Bergsson 1991
Translation copyright © Bernard Scudder 1997

Cover image by Jethro, Squid Inc.
Original cover design by Börkur Arnarson
Typeset by Agnesi Text Hadleigh Suffolk
Printed and bound by Antony Rowe Ltd Chippenham Wiltshire

ISBN 1 899197 35 4

Svanurinn was originally published in Iceland by Forlagid, Reykjavík, 1991. This translation is published by agreement with Forlagid.

Mare's Nest Publishing is pleased to acknowledge the assistance of the Fund for the Translation of Icelandic Literature.

This publication has been facilitated by the generous participation of the Icelandic Embassy, London.

This book is published with the financial assistance of the Arts Council of England.

The Swan

Gudbergur Bergsson

Translated from the Icelandic
by Bernard Scudder

MARE'S NEST

1

The moment the coach set off, the girl started to miss the rock and the sea, and her sense of loss grew all the more painful after they reached where the grass grows, the birds sing, the river flows and the sun glitters on ponds and marshes. Alongside the road were ditches with water in and tall grass growing on their banks. When she sat at the coach window watching the grasslands passing by she resolved always to think of the sea that summer when she was on her own. This was the way she was thinking as the coach drove progressively farther from the sea and the clouds sent swift shadows across the land. The grey shadows passed over the grass and it turned dark green in an instant, then regained its normal colour. Into the sunshine a hint of sorrow crept afterwards which the shadows, flat plains and vastness magnified. This was not the vastness of the sea but of an earth that was growing ever larger, since one piece of land took over from another and the coach seemed as if it would never reach its destination for all the mountains, marshes and rivers. It drove along a road that turned into other, innumerable roads. Some lay across high bridges, and then she would try to glance quickly down into the water that swirled into eddies and grew so deep that it reached into her mind with terror. She closed her eyes, sensed the deep pool and opened them again at once, to stop herself vanishing into the river beneath the wheels of the coach and the bridges.

The girl knew that in the countryside there was supposed to be a white river with a strong current, and she tried to turn it into sea on her way there in the coach. This didn't work, because the sea was endless, wide and green, but the river just a long, slender strip of water in her mind. It was so different from the sea, which is uncrossable.

You could cross the river, by both bridge and boat, to say nothing of the mind, even though it eventually flowed out into the blue. She knew that the river ceased to be a river in the end and became open sea. Because it stops flowing. Instead, it turns choppy, depending upon the way the storms blow.

When she left, her mother had accompanied her to the coach terminal and said, 'This is the first time you go away from your home to the countryside, away from your parents, so try to like things there. Be polite and well-behaved towards everyone, and then you'll forget what you did. And when you come back home, everyone else will have forgotten it too.'

Then she took her in her arms and whispered, 'We enjoy forgetting as much as remembering, my dear.'

Before her father went to work that morning he had said to her, as they got dressed together for the first time, 'If you make a good impression the farmer might let you stay on to help him for the whole winter and pay you wages.'

He had hardly spoken those words before her mouth and throat filled up with soft, dry rock, a peculiar gravel that she could swallow only with a huge effort.

Afterwards they started talking plainly about how much she would grow up and develop in the countryside, how the air there was much healthier than in town and the people carefree and good-natured.

'Even if it's maybe not entirely like that, you ought to believe it is all the same,' said her father.

A vague impression came over her, strange and welcome in the morning light, of grass, animals, mountains and people, radiating a glow. This was a feeling she tried to avoid, just like crying.

The girl was at once relieved and sad. She could feel this on the coach, and inhaled deeply while it drove past the houses. Afterwards she whispered to herself, because the journey was an endless moment of farewell, 'Never, never. The coach will never go past this cliff again, and I shall never again see that brown bird that is flying away now, and I shall never drive past this mountain. I only see it once in a lifetime, now and never again.'

A sensation crept into her eyes that she was gradually dying, the farther the coach drove along the road.

'And if I do ever go back, when I'm big, this bird won't be there to welcome me. It'll be dead long ago, without ever having known that I sat on a coach once and saw it. I'll probably have forgotten this cliff, the mountain, even the sea. On the way back home I shall not see exactly what I saw on the route from home. Because the coach will be travelling in the opposite direction from the one it is driving now, and I shall see everything differently and think that the cliff is a new cliff, the mountain another mountain. I shall be big and everything will be much smaller and lower than when I left. Going back will be different from going away, even though the road is the same, the road that leads from home and back home.'

At the same time she began to bid farewell through the window to everything she was seeing for the last time. She felt she was withering and dying in the sunshine with wisps of cloud scudding over the land. She rode like this from the sea's waves to green, arched hills.

When the coach had driven past the outermost houses they became a memory that she held on to, but they were sucked down into a haze and she could hardly call them back to mind. It was as if the houses and the people inside them had died upon her driving away. Everything died the farther she went. Even her house back home was somehow left hanging in the air, like a vague vision, after the countryside had taken over.

The birds flying over the grass were light and small, not as attentive as the ponderous, broad-winged sea birds. They would fly up suddenly away from the coach, more like sounds, frightened screeches, than real birds. They were completely different from the gulls that had the ocean in their feathers and swung it out of them towards the sky. Flying through the air, they would flap their wings in the same way that the sea lifted slow waves. Their eyes were clocks that measure no time. But the darting little birds did not think. They were like little stones that an invisible being or spirit had hurled brutally up out of the ground.

The farther the coach drove on, the clearer it became that there was no way of turning back. The moisture of the sea had disappeared from the wind that blew in through the half-open window. In some places, the land was showing the first signs of spring as it turned green and the gusts of wind conveyed an unsalty, strange moisture of soil growing warmer. For as far as the eye could see there was the tranquillity of the land, not the soothing, mysterious sigh that the sea gives off when the heavy spring calm spreads over it after a winter of crashing waves. The earth comes to life in spring, but the sea dies at the same time, or hibernates. It comes to resemble a blue, ever-moving, fluid animal that lies calm. All the same, it has its eyes about it, ready to flare up hissing against the shore.

The girl saw the green-blue animal in her imagination but did not know what species it could be. It was a cross between a monster and faithful domestic animal, but kneaded together from water and born of dreams. That sort of animal was easier to sense than to see.

Suddenly she began to whimper inaudibly to herself. She whimpered at everything she saw. She made prolonged, silent whimpers, with the palm of her hand over her mouth, as if she were singing, and she watched the countryside, the farms and meadows that certain men owned and no one else. They were called farmers. But everyone shared the sea, no one could settle on it or send their animals out on it to graze. No one could own the sea, because it flows incessantly up into the sky and back down to itself invisibly, through the sun and rain.

'No one can own the sea any more than human love, just like no one can own you even if he marries you and takes you for his own and you take him for your own,' her father had said.

The girl whimpered silently, her mind on what she sensed, without making a sound, but remained sitting still with her back straight while the coach proceeded mercilessly on its way.

Sometimes it would stop. People got off and others boarded and rode a short way with it. Dogs ran from the farms down slopes and meadows, either to snap or to welcome the people who alighted. The girl felt no joy at seeing the unrestrained joy of the dogs. She knew that no one would rejoice when she finally reached her destination, not even a dog.

It was obvious that the man the dogs were welcoming was well and truly home. His smile showed that he could tell this from their toadying to him, but he ordered them to stop for form's sake.

That's how the land was different from the sea.

The girl knew that even if she were to go straight back home and walk down to the beach, no fish would swim up to the shore to welcome her arrival by flipping its tail. No one welcomes anyone who walks down to the sea. Anyone who does that feels only the sense of welcome in his own breast at meeting again the wet expanse of the ocean that was left behind when he went.

'That's the difference between the sea and the land,' she thought.

2

Suddenly the girl felt in her breast that unlimited toughness which is constantly on the verge of turning into water, but which you keep under control while other people can see and are near by. You conceal the transformation until you are alone and no one can see how you turn blind down in your own depths and somehow remote from yourself and others. You listen and peep at the same time. For precisely that reason she sat in silence all the way, gathering what she intended to digest later and sob out of her system by herself, and felt that she was travelling in a cage on wheels.

One of the passengers who was sitting in front of her began singing in a loud voice about the countryside, the sun and the soil, while a fair maid drank her ale. Before her eyes, and suddenly audible to her ears, was what had previously existed only in poems and stories that she had read in school textbooks. She was on the trail of material for poems. What she saw was fine to look at through the window to musical accompaniment, had she never needed to reach her destination and associate with any of it in an unfamiliar place.

Over her settled a dim haze from the mountain which unexpectedly erupts with sadness somewhere within the person who leaves home for the first time. And she lay beneath it for the rest of the journey.

The coach stopped, the driver looked over his shoulder, turned his gaze vacantly upon her and said, 'This is where you're supposed to get out. Someone's here to fetch you.'

At these words she looked out and saw the farmer for the first time. He was waiting alone on the road and there was no house in sight, just the drive behind him which vanished between two fairly low hills.

As soon as she stepped out of the coach, her legs stiff, she could hear the sound of the birds and somehow also the slow vegetation. Life she had never heard before resounded everywhere from the distance of lakes and grasslands. It seemed to be carried from all directions at once, up from the earth and out of the sky. Two different sounds merged in her ears. It was different from when she heard the sound of the sky and the surf against the cliffs. That sound had drowned out everything with its roaring and the land fell silent at the same instant. The murmuring of the sea was that sound itself and the shore remained quiet in its silence.

The driver had jumped out before her and jerked her suitcase hurriedly out from the luggage compartment and slammed it down by the roadside. Everything he did was jerky. He slung the suitcase down at the farmer's feet. Before she even greeted him the girl looked him in the eye, because her mother had urged her to do so and said, 'Look him straight in the eye before you greet him. You haven't got a thief's eyes.'

'The suitcase, here,' said the driver and jerked himself back into the coach and drove jerkily away.

The farmer was wearing his working clothes: a blue Mao suit, with the jacket much more faded than the trousers. The back of it was almost white. The sun had eaten away the colour while he was stooped over his work. Then he asked, 'Can't you lift the suitcase yourself?'

'Yes,' she said. 'But I can't carry it very far.'

They had forgotten to greet each other properly with a handshake, or did so somehow fumblingly when they touched the handle of the suitcase.

'So you're strong then,' he said, and produced a piece of string from his pocket and tied it around the suitcase, even though the lock was secure. Then he swung it effortlessly on to his back and wriggled it better up on to his shoulders.

'Oh, it's not heavy,' he said, smiling as if pleased to have been given a burden to put on his back.

The suitcase was not heavy, but still the farmer always kept his eyes on the ground. As he walked he seemed to be monitoring his

7

every footstep, checking carefully how he placed one foot in front of the other, so as not to stumble on the smooth road. He did not introduce himself, but was clearly the master of the farm.

'Follow along behind me,' he said. 'It's just a short way back and no place for a car. We'll just walk there.'

Instead of following him, she walked a little way in front, slightly to one side of him, occasionally glancing over her shoulder. He was licking his lips then; he often licked his dry lips but kept silent and did not slow down. In the dip between the hills she saw that the farm was a short distance ahead, on a gentle slope or a hill, and suddenly there was deathly silence all around them. The farmer's even, plodding but effortless steps on the track intensified the silence. The sun intensified, too, and its light illuminated the tranquillity. When they emerged from the hills to face the plain, the girl thought she would suffocate in the vastness of it all. A feeling of apprehension crept up on her. Nature was so tremendously huge, she so minute. And she could hardly move, even though she was safe to run about at liberty there, free from any traffic danger. Yet she did not run. She knew that she had gone out to the vastness to other people who would restrict her movements with duties, and she let the farmer overtake her and walked behind him.

They met a man on the road. The farmer stopped and stood bowed beneath the suitcase while they spoke together. Although he was talking to the man, it was as if he were talking to no one, to his toes or to the earth. The girl did not understand what they were discussing, except that they were talking about animals. The farmer did not sweat beneath his burden, but he often scratched his chin by rubbing it against the corner of the bag that projected over his shoulder. Then he would pull a face.

She looked around while they stood there talking. Along the side of the road was quite a deep ditch, and water in it with a colourful brown slick on the surface. The soil on the banks was almost red. When she looked around more carefully she noticed that the vastness was not unbroken, but dissected by ditches. Yet it was not an ocean of marshes and lakes; rather it did not commit itself about whether it

8

was sea or land. It was treacherous wetland. Only the road was secure underfoot, and lay across the marshes. The longer she looked in all directions, the more she saw how disturbing the vastness could be, even though it ended in mountains in the distance. It offered no obstacles to the eyes and the sight, but was difficult to negotiate for the feet.

At this thought, she was seized by the sensation that she was lifting up or soaring to a vertiginous height and would soon crash down and be swallowed by the earth. She felt slightly nauseous and for safety's sake she rubbed the soles of her shoes on the road which lay like a thin line from the main road to the farms around her. Then the farmers began exchanging their farewells and one of them said, 'Perhaps you'll keep an eye on the animals for me.'

Then all of a sudden he asked, 'Is that the girl who's coming to stay with you?'

'Yes,' said the one with the suitcase.

They went their separate ways without exchanging any other words. Then a dog jumped unexpectedly out from a ditch and followed the girl and the farmer. Before she knew it, dogs had arrived from everywhere. One even seemed to crawl out from beneath a stone. They followed the man with the suitcase. The one that had emerged from the ditch was wet, muddy, panting for breath and acted as if it owned the farmer, who began to talk to it and chastised it good-naturedly. The dog let its tongue hang down in delight at being told off.

The girl was seized by boredom. Her mind felt disdain for the furry animals. And now the ewes that were standing grazing at the roadside began to look up one after the other and watch the farmer strolling past them. He called out something to them and they immediately began to bleat and defecate, while the dog shook its head in delight.

'This is healthy, innocent rural joy,' she thought, but even the shy birds did not arouse her joy. They flew up from the tussocks that were sallow with thick dry grass, and from the clumps of grass along the roadside, and startled her.

Suddenly the dog stuck its nose out into the wind which stroked its hair and combed it back. It sniffed at the vastness and closed its eyes.

'Uh-huh,' said the farmer, moistening his lips.

The dog seemed to understand this and started barking furiously. The girl began wishing that the road was endless, she would never have to leave it and head for the farm, that it ended nowhere and her journey was a mere drawing on a sketchpad: her, the farmer, the dogs, the sun, the ewes, the farmhouse and the countryside all around. If it were, she would erase it at once. But they drew steadily closer to the buildings. Soon afterwards there was nothing left of the road and a woman with a cold, clammy hand greeted them.

'Hello,' she said. 'Are you the new girl then?'

The farmer put the suitcase down on the ground and kept his mouth open, even though he was not out of breath in the slightest. The girl expected him to take off his cap and scratch the top of his head, but he just sighed and asked for some coffee.

'Eh,' he said, and added a few sounds.

'Why didn't you fetch her in the car?' asked the woman, and showed the girl into a room with two beds. She pointed to one of them and said, 'That's your sack.'

The farmer sized up the suitcase, then slid it under one of the beds. There was no mistaking the fact that she was in the countryside. Her mother had said that suitcases were always kept under the beds there, and when they were pulled out again, they had fluff on them from the sheet. 'It was like that when I worked on a farm and it's sure to be the same now. That's one thing in the countryside that will never change.'

The afternoon dragged on and the girl spent most of the time sitting on the bed. She tried to breathe quietly so as not to frighten off the calm. The farmer and his wife seemed to have died. There was no sign of them. Time passed without the slightest audible sign of life. She crept cautiously to the window and saw that the dog was asleep with its nose over one of its paws. Time passed in a static progress. She could tell by her watch that it was passing and the sun went past the windows on two sides of the house. Evening did not really come, but it had come all the same. Then suddenly the farmer's wife appeared and asked in surprise, 'Are you sitting here instead of going out? On your day off too.'

The girl heaved a sigh, relieved at being able to stand up from the bed and move about unhindered.

After dinner, the evening turned into huge fiery-red jaws on the ceiling to the west. The girl hovered around the farm like a tongue which had no appetite to taste the environment at dusk. The farmer's wife looked at her inquisitively when she found her sitting on the bed again.

'Don't let your backside get glued to the quilt, because you'll not be much use for work then and I'll tan your hide,' she joked.

The girl glanced towards the window. She saw the evening tranquillity outside and heard the sound of a car fade away. The farmer and his wife had popped out somewhere and left her there by herself. She thought without thinking, 'This place is welcome to itself for all I care.'

Then she began undressing and hovered in the air for a while between sleep and the waking state. When she returned from her flight, before falling asleep, she decided to dream about her house back home. She resolved to stay there in future while she slept at night, even if she did have to work while she was awake during the day, perhaps for the rest of her life.

But she dreamed something quite different from what she had resolved. A strange receptacle rolled in through the door of a large house which was full of bobbins after an incomprehensible event had taken place, when she met a man whom she had never seen. Then nothing else happened in her sleep that night.

3

When the girl woke up there was no definite time in the light. It was neither morning, nor evening, nor the middle of the day. And she had no idea where she was, whether it was in the present, yesterday, today or some other time which she did not know. The light was alien, originating in a different world from the one she was used to, and out of it walked a woman who slipped through a door into her chest.

Soon she got her bearings and everything shrank back inside herself. She knew where she was and at the same time noticed the smell of wet earth, animals and an unfamiliar house. It was the crack of dawn, long before she was accustomed to waking up at home. That was why she did not recognize the light. The woman had driven her out of her sleep. After initial surprise, bewilderment and the timelessness of the light, the mercilessness awoke which would later shroud everything from morning to evening.

Immediately on the first day she became unfamiliar to herself. It was not she who was staying at this place. For the first time she felt how easy it was to conceal loss and sorrow in the mind, without anyone noticing. Even when people were watching, they did not watch in order to see, and so she realized that being alone was being among strangers and wanting to be that way.

She was not assigned any particular job to do as soon as she had got up and had her breakfast, but she was kept under mild supervision. She was not allowed out and had to be ready to lend a hand in the kitchen. She sat there on a wooden bench and said nothing.

Even the food tasted different from the food at home. Everything was different: the light, the taste, the smell, the sight and the feeling. The white milk hurt her eyes. The curds gave off an uncomfortable cold. The spoon was made of harder metal than those back home, and it had a hostile poisonous taste. There was nothing around her except sheer cold, the clarity of silence, but there was turbulence and smoke in them both all the same. The farmer's wife had said, 'Have a decent breakfast, then you'll feel good.'

There was a smell of dogs in the house, a strong animal scent everywhere, from the farmer's wife and the farmer too. The girl remembered her mother saying, 'In the countryside, everything smells of dogs' arses.'

Everything was clean and neat and tidy indoors, but when she inhaled the smell of the farm she was on the verge of choking, so she crept out to the hallway to the front door with her mouth wide open, as if intending to suck in the surroundings. She held down the fresh air for a while, then coughed it back up.

Somehow she still managed to adapt to the countryside this way. 'Four months,' she thought. 'No longer.' Then she went back into the kitchen, sat down on the bench and waited for something, not knowing what it might be. She just waited.

A little while later a boy from the next farm burst in and when he saw her he said all in a rush, 'Come out and play, it's such good weather.'

He was tidy and smartly dressed. His face was like whipped cream, but with strawberry colouring on his cheeks. He tried to pin his smile on everything, while chirping into himself the way that fat little boys do without laughing candidly. The cause was absolute well-being and he writhed in bright, plump fat.

'She didn't come here to play,' the farmer's wife answered quickly. 'She's supposed to work.'

To emphasize her words she ordered the girl to take the rubbish out. The boy's chirping suddenly stopped, while he watched the girl in disappointment and his smile waned. He seemed totally uncomprehending and she walked silently round him, giving him a wide berth. Then he jumped back to life and writhed some more, but still backed away. His chirping started again. The girl felt a vast difference between them when the farmer's wife asked quite sharply and sarcastically, 'Don't your parents pay to have you on the farm?'

The fat little boy admitted it and his eyes turned sad. His dimples and the strawberries on his cheeks grew pale.

Never before had the girl felt any difference between herself and other children. Now she knew that the wall existed and that she was only herself, not like other children, just her alone and herself. This made her parents into people remote from her, too, and the same went for her brother and sister, her grandfather and grandmother. The woman's quick, relentless words had cut them off from her while the girl was struggling into the hallway and outdoors with the rubbish bin. If she hadn't been carrying something heavy she would certainly have tumbled head over heels, poured the rubbish over herself and started crying, completely abandoned, but the bin was so heavy that the struggling and concentration to prevent it spilling kept her mind and body in balance. She pulled a face to hide how upset she was.

'Spread the rubbish out for the chickens beside the cabbage patch!' the farmer's wife called after her. 'They can peck at it then.'

The boy started writhing again, ran ahead of her and said, 'I know where to throw the rubbish away, I'll show you.'

She spread out the rubbish in front of the chickens, and they ran straight for it. The boy made no move while she did so. Then all of a sudden he said, 'It pays to be like you, not like me.'

She gave him an inquisitive look, and he added, 'Maybe you'll get paid some money in the autumn, since they're not paid to have you here. I know I won't get anything.'

She looked at him.

'You'll make some money,' said the boy. 'Because you're supposed to work.'

She went on looking at him.

'Your parents will make money on you,' he added excitedly. 'My mum and dad lose on me. This is the second summer they've lost on me.'

She looked away, feeling sorry for both the boy and his parents.

'Can't you see the difference between us?' he asked, adding, 'Can't you speak?'

The chickens clucked around them. The girl was about to open her mouth and make a sound, but did not know what to say. She merely cleared her throat. When the boy ran off she tried to clear the silence out of herself with words.

'Sure I can speak,' she said.

Her voice was normal and low. Because of the unexpected joy that seized her, she started clucking in competition with the chickens. Sometimes they all clucked in chorus. It was as if there were an animal inside her that could cluck, low, bleat and neigh, as if she could do it by instinct. Then she put her hand over her mouth.

'We've got a new little chicken,' the farmer's wife said merrily when she returned with the empty bin. 'You'll soon fit in to the country-side. Animals are helpful to children.'

She had grown friendly.

The girl closed her eyes for a moment to conjure up a mental image which was different from the woman's kindness. It was of her mother. She was doing the washing. A thick cloud of steam wafted out of the door of the washing machine, concealing her. She stored her mother away there, then opened her eyes and smiled. From now on she planned to pretend all the time and play for the whole summer, so that she could play like the boy, but in her own way, differently from him. It was the end of May. She had been sent to the country-side, to a good farm with people who would annul what she had done. And she was supposed to work for her keep.

While she was standing in front of the farmer's smiling wife she suddenly sent invisible poison out of her head and around the whole house. She poisoned the rooms, the people, the animals, the plants and the air, but smiled all the same and asked, 'What should I do next?'

4

Straight away the next day the girl was sent out to the marsh to fetch a horse which the farmer had said was blue dun. She didn't know what this might be but suspected that blue dun was a colour, although she did not ask for fear of being considered stupid.

Then she set off slowly, in doubt, down the meadow with the bridle over her shoulder. This was the first time she had left the home-fields and looked forward to being by herself, in the hope that the answer would have easier access to her out in the open than near to the house, and that, if it was a colour, it would enter her mind like a flash.

'Blue dun: what's that?' she thought, fully prepared to encounter the answer.

The horses were grazing a vast distance away on the marshland. Seen from so far away in bright sunshine, the horses were unreal, in another world of wondrously beautiful apprehension in her body and they shone in the glittering distance. Sometimes the horses seemed to be lifting up from the earth, as if the air were swirling them around in a heavy, billowing silver stream, and somehow erasing them or part of them. Without a moment's warning, legless or headless horses would be hovering around in the rippling calm. There was clear sunshine in the grass and all over the sky. It was as if a moist heat had suddenly been poured out of a blue dome.

She had hardly set foot outside the meadow on to the hummocky marsh before everything began to bounce and dance beneath her feet. It was not firm earth, but rather stiff jelly in slight motion. Her feet half disappeared into reddish slush and she smelt the stench of rusty old iron from it. The brown marsh water splashed with a slurp on to her boots. The earth whined beneath her feet, the mud spat with a brutal growl from under her soles and the bog seemed about to swallow her, but did not; her feet always stopped at a certain depth. And her fear waned the farther she made it across that peculiar mixture of air, mud and water. In a while she started to enjoy this farce, when her feet were sucked downwards by an unknown force, and she jerked them back up with her own force and will. The soil yielded and it wheezed when she vanquished the slush. 'Plop, plop-plop,' said the marsh with every step she took.

She plodded on like this over the wet ground and soon grew tired, being unaccustomed to supple earth.

The horses always seemed to be as far away, no matter how she tried to hurry. The slightly undulating flatland seemed to lengthen the distance with every step. Mirages rippled the air. But she could see through it, how pure, innocent and clear it was. At her feet, a swarm of flies buzzed constantly over the grass.

Then suddenly she had reached the horses, but then it was the horses that slowly retreated before her on the waves of air. They did not stop grazing, but glanced askance at her showing the whites of their eyes and swished their tails scornfully at her and at the flies. She felt their mockery and irritation at her for not knowing anything about horses, and not even being able to tell their colours apart. In fact they all seemed alike to her or in all colours of the rainbow except blue. She had only ever seen a horse that colour once, in a picture.

One horse did not shy away. It stood still, apparently waiting, and she approached it rather hesitantly. Then it looked up, lifted its head high with its ears cocked, its lips moist with green grass, looked at her as a holy being would have done and stood completely still while she put the bridle on it the way the farmer had done, when he taught her to bridle a horse; he pretended to put the bridle on her, saying with a menacing laugh, 'That's the way you'd be bridled by a good farmer if you were a mare.'

The bridle fitted effortlessly on to the horse's head as if put there by magic and the bit found its way into its mouth without the slightest resistance. For an instant her hands seemed to grow wings by slipping the bridle into the horse's mouth which was full of hot, foaming green from the grass. It all went smoothly, the horse was like a well-behaved child helping to dress itself. She led it home behind her by the reins.

When she reached the farm, the farmer was waiting and asked why she hadn't ridden the horse.

'Aren't you always supposed to lead horses?' she asked.

He laughed and she thought he was going to make her take the horse back, because she had surely fetched one of the wrong colour. But he didn't, and she tried to memorize the colour so that she would know what a blue dun horse looked like. 'Blue dun is that colour,' she repeated to herself several times. 'It's not any definite colour, but it's the colour of a certain horse. It's a brownish grey.' She was pleased at how easy it had been to find and fetch a blue dun horse. 'Maybe horses of that colour are easiest to fetch,' she thought. Somehow they seemed to put their bridles on themselves.

The farmer said it was best to let her mount the horse to see whether she could sit on it, and he lifted her on to its back at once.

'We'll see,' he said, with a laconic expression.

What am I supposed to do now?

She sat insecure and trembling on the horse, at a previously unknown distance from everything, ethereal, slightly apprehensive and giddy, but none the less rejoicing and triumphant within herself. For an instant she thought her stomach would slip out through her mouth like an inflated purple balloon. There had to be a fish darting somewhere in her innards, because in her stomach she could feel the flipping tail of a fish that gave off a groaning sound; it did not seem to know which end of her to shoot out of.

Suddenly, without her knowing why, she dug her feet hard and firm into the sides of the horse, which rushed off down the slope, and she was thrown off its back. As she fell, something swirled away from her in fragments: the houses by the shore, the sea and her playmates, her vision went black and she tumbled on to the grass and into the world of animals. Eventually she stopped rolling uncontrollably in the cool grass and lay on her back looking up at the sky. As if in a trance, she had the notion that she had just died and was looking for the first time up into pale blue eternity with a few clouds on it, but at the same moment the farmer jolted her to her feet out of this peaceful sensation.

'That will teach you that animals are sensitive,' he said. 'You've got to get a feel for them.'

She had not sustained any injuries and could stand on her feet. Even her neck was all right, because the farmer said, 'No, your neck's not broken. People don't always break their necks falling off horses. It sometimes happens though. But you're too young, your bones are supple.'

And her head hadn't flown off!

The farmer's wife warmed to her, welcomed her as if she had tumbled from the horse and into the life of the household and become valid by the act of falling from horseback. That evening when she went to sleep, everything did not vanish into a haze around her. This was unlike what had happened on the first night, when she had never been to sleep in unfamiliar surroundings before.

She felt uncomfortable but sweet pains in her body. No sooner had she put her tired head on the pillow than she merged with the breathing of someone who had not yet arrived but would come the following day and doubtless sleep in the other bed tomorrow night. She had heard the farmer and his wife talking about it. She was thinking about this and was unaware when sleep made her merge with the quiet outside the window, the chill, the grass and the breeze.

In her sleep it was as if she were lying awake or sleep were another type of wakefulness, a much more tender wakefulness than the one you wake up to and toil away in by day. The disturbing corpse smell of the dogs had gone. She did not start from sleep afraid that wakeful flies were hovering around her room in the twilight and settling with tickly feet on her mouth and nose. Before then, they had made the night seem both shorter and longer with their continuous harassment. They smelt of dogs and cows' urine. Now, fatigue did not allow them to exist any more. Her body melted into sleep and flowed over the earth, marshes and mountains, until the fatigue left it and it shrank back once more to its normal size. Then she dreamt that a dream was growing out of her whole body. She grasped for it suddenly with her fingers and felt long hairs standing out of her body everywhere in huge brushes, and out of her eyes and fingers too. Then it grew so quickly that it covered her all over, making her a tiny bump in the clump of hair, and she thought in desperation, 'I shall never escape from here.'

She woke panting for breath in a new day. But she was not tired in the slightest and she touched herself cautiously all over in search of the hair. Then she could tell in the morning light that she knew she was definitely awake and no longer in a dream.

5

The birds had aroused a feeling of wonder and fear within her, because the earth seemed to be clearing a path for her by tossing them suddenly up into the air from beneath her feet, to stop her tripping over them. Unexpectedly, all of a sudden, they shot up in front of her, brown whining pebbles with their wings flapping furiously. She tried to avoid being hit by this soft shower of stones. Once she had grown used to them, the birds springing up from their hiding places made her jump and set her heart pounding, but she enjoyed both sensations all the same and started scouting around for them. Their colour matched the earth so closely that she never noticed them until they shot up. The pained whine of the winged bird of rock aroused rejoicing, greed, yearning to find their nests, to deprive the birds of their secrecy; but she could never find them.

Country birds did not seem to make their nests in fixed places year after year like the birds back home. There they were in a definite place, either in trees or holes in walls. In the countryside there were countless hiding places and the grass grew over the nests, concealing them. Some kind of secrecy and silence lay over everything here.

When she walked through the outfields she was seized by the repulsive, ticklish sensation that the roots of the sallow grass whose blades peeped up from the tussocks were chock-a-block with wriggling chicks, so that sometimes she hardly dared to put her foot down, and felt a tingle pass through her body and the sinful notion that she was crushing a bird's egg or squashing a little half-feathered chick beneath the soles of her shoes. None the less, as with everything else, she grew accustomed to her feet sinking into the sallow grass just as they did into the marsh, and perhaps trampling an egg or a chick to pulp.

In the countryside, the earth seemed as insecure under foot as it was natural to live and die on.

In a short time she had been forced to take stock of various unexpected occurrences. Normal sleep had taken its time coming to her, because when she slept she turned a different way from at home. This seemed to confuse her body about which way to point when entering sleep, and her mind dithered uneasily because of the changed direction of its dreams.

The first thing she had done when she went outside on the first day was to try to realize clearly which direction she ought to look and turn if she wondered about home or directed her thoughts there, to make sure that the thoughts would definitely reach their destination. The direction was southwest. But she could not see the entire route, only a short way, because not far on the other side of the river was a high mountain that rose up against her thoughts and blocked her view.

The mountain was doubtless higher than it looked, and the peak was therefore generally hidden under a white-grey hat of clouds. Her questions about it met a muted response, but she was told there was a big lake on top of it, like many mountains in the district, and they were all joined up by tunnels with underground rivers cascading through them, and according to folklore a monster moved among the mountains and lived in the depths of the lakes and could sometimes be seen swimming in the guise of a swan on their immaculately smooth surfaces, in the absolute and paralysing tranquillity of the highlands.

Local people had a custom of riding up to the mountain once every summer, in early August, in the hope of seeing the swan soar out of the deep, draped with plants and weeds, and up to the surface, singing of the character and fate of whoever beheld it. Nowadays, no one could be bothered any more to climb up and throw something into the lake, preferably a flower or stone from where they lived, to startle out its white but demonic secret, so the swan would reveal what it knew about other people.

'Those old wives' tales are a thing of the past,' the farmer's wife said. 'But it's fun for kids to go on horseback near the end of summer, if only to give themselves a healthy old fright outdoors in nature.'

These words sent a spasm through the girl's chest and at once she started waiting for the day of the trek. She knew how much ecstasy fright can bring, when it has almost passed by with its sticky spread wings coming loose from the stiff body. That is a wonderful reincarnation. And this was the reason she enjoyed stealing so much, especially from shops, feeling her heart pound and then being alone with her booty in her hiding place, but never entirely safe. It was like imagining a cosmic war and horrendous death while lying in a comfortable bed. She never felt so fond of her parents as when she had watched horror films on television or seen terrified people running half naked and weeping through burning, wet, devastated city streets on newsreels.

But perhaps her love or fondness was not directed at anything in particular.

She decided to be quick about learning to sit a horse properly, so that she could go on the trek with the children, and she waited in suspense for the day when they would go off to the mountain. Usually a red hue crept into the clouds over the mountain in the evenings. In her mind, they piled up over the world at sunset. A sense of loss akin to infinity seized her before the peace of night descended, even seeming to threaten the dogs. They were seized by fear at the calmness and beauty of the earth, for they would let out occasional frightened yaps and growl at nothing in particular. The dogs' barking in the evenings was a fearful ode to the night that seemed to arrive innocent, contemplative, transparent, clad in light veils.

At this time of year the night resembled an endless thought about nothing at all. It was vacuous, a futile memory far removed from what it had resolved upon and had been essential in daylight: that every object had a purpose in its place. Night was just a thought in itself and did not extend beyond its own limits, since it was nocturnal brightness over the whole world. And the night thought its vacuous, transparent thought about itself until morning, when the sun rose from the wetlands in the east and gradually lifted the lakes from the firm earth and made them unearthly. The night thought vanished and then the time had come to turn away from nonsense, out of the trance, and off to do some hard physical labour.

The girl drove the cows out in the bright morning, in the golden and green speckles given off by the grass, where tiny pointless and harmless flies were swarming. She yawned as they buzzed around her; the cows' tails swung rhythmically to dodge what dripped out; and in a comfortable tiredness that wanted to drag her in exhaustion into new sleep among the tussocks, she racked her numbed brains about why the cow pats resembled little brown and round slabs of newly flowed lava. The smell, too, was similar to that sometimes given off by sun-baked stones among rotting seaweed.

Every place has its own distinctive smell, even though that smell is always the same. The cows plodded along to the meadow, and she plodded along too in her ridiculous imaginings, thinking that they ought to have thick wool instead of hides.

Idling away the time, she had the sudden notion of investigating whether poppies were called dream-flowers because of a particular dream inside them. To find out, she tore up a few and waited in suspense for night. Just before bedtime she hid herself away to chew them and went to bed straight afterwards to receive their dreams beneath her quilt. For a moment a sweet dream about nothing descended upon her, woven from a finely meshed net. Then it vanished and did not return no matter how she lay afterwards in grassy hollows, chewing and eating dream-flowers in the hope of recapturing the dream.

But when she looked at the flowers around her they still brought her a pleasure akin to sleep. She knew what only a few of them were called. Gradually she learned the names of the commonest ones, and with such knowledge the nameless flowers grew most beautiful of all in her eyes. If she found nameless, beautiful flowers she committed the place to memory so that she could go back there to see them, but found neither the place nor the flowers the following day. Either the flowers lived for only one day or they could change their appearance at night and hide themselves from her sight, to prevent her picking them. Then she perceived how vague everything in nature is, how multiple and concealed.

The farmhand who arrived to work there seemed to turn a blind eye to everything but his work even though he had spent several summers there before, and she did so too in a certain sense, and listened to him talking on familiar terms to the farmer and his wife. Sometimes he watched television in silence with them. It showed continually crumbling cities and children running through their ruins. She envied them for having so many ruins with countless holes like mysterious caves to play and hide in, where there were doubtless people who were dead for real, corpses and ghosts.

'You shouldn't watch those awful scenes, they're not for children,' the farmer's wife said. 'You ought to be reading about something beautiful in a good children's book instead.'

Reading was the last thing she wanted to do. If she was not allowed to watch these scenes on television she imagined them as being much more horrific than they were: children running around with the veins standing out of their bodies and blood spitting ceaselessly from them on to burning houses. Everything stank of burning blood. She lay half paralysed on her bed, thinking about the fire-brigade children with all their bloody hoses with jets spurting from them, until the farmer and his wife returned home, if they had gone out to pay calls with the farmhand in the evenings after work. Then she undressed in silence and fell into a gentle sleep in the brightness of night.

All the same, she would try to read a book if the television was switched off, but the story took such a long time to happen in print that she yielded to the swift profusion that was rushing through her own mind. If she tried to hurry the story along and help it to turn into something enjoyable, by glossing over words, the action would disintegrate and the story would become incomprehensible; but that was often the best part. And if her mind flew ahead of the action it turned out much more trite than she had imagined when she finally reached it after great exertion, countless words and boring sentences.

The book she tried to read, called *The Island of Happiness*, kept her mind best occupied, try as it would to head off and change the story as it saw fit. The farmer's wife sometimes asked her what she had been reading about now, and if she answered as best she could, the woman would say in astonishment, 'Yes, but there's nothing about that in the book. I've read it myself.'

The girl grew confused at remembering something completely different from what she had read. Finally she put the book down, convinced that she did not know the proper way to read. She did not even want to learn to read properly, after the farmer's wife had told her what the book was actually about. Perhaps she would hold a book to please the farmer's wife, and let her gaze rest idly on the lines or follow them for appearance's sake, but she was not going to read anything.

'But you can read, can't you?' the farmer said, apparently interested by the fact that she would read or seem to read books but remember something other than the actual story. He intended to teach her to remember what she read, but she started to cry under his interrogation.

He made her read out loud and she did so reluctantly, then he asked her and she remembered the story correctly, but if she read in silence or without guidance it would come back out of her topsy-turvy or unrecognizable, and so strange that he rolled around laughing, sometimes even finding her version better, but worse at the same time because it was completely wrong in comparison with the text.

'You really come out of a different world after you've been reading,' he laughed.

She did not reply.

Then he asked cautiously, 'Do you read differently to yourself from when you read out loud for other people?'

'Yes,' she answered, but began to doubt whether what she read was always the same and not constantly playing hide-and-seek like beauty and the flowers that could never be found in the grassy hollows the day after she had found them.

'The point isn't to be able to read, or to read books,' said the farmer's wife, 'but to be able to repeat things correctly and know what's right and what's wrong. You don't seem to know that, not in this case or any other. But hopefully it'll all work out this summer and you'll learn the difference between right and wrong. Otherwise you'll be a miscreant in everything you do.'

The girl started crying again.

The farmer tested her several times, dumbfounded at discovering that when she was asked or told to answer, she would always repeat correctly what he had said, even the day after he had read aloud to her and she to him; but, as before, no one could recognize the books that she read to herself in silence.

'You're a fluent reader,' the farmer said. 'Maybe you read a story in your mind that's different from what it says on the page. It can't seem to find its way through all the stuff that's in your head already. People who live by the coast are sometimes like that.'

The moment he said this, she visualized the endless sea and said brutally, 'We don't need to read.'

'Why not?' he asked.

She didn't know the reason this was unnecessary.

'Do you want to be empty-headed?' he asked.

She bit her lip, blinked her eyes and cleared her throat.

'You just clear your throat,' he said. 'But in life, that's not enough for your mouth and your wits to get by with, unless you're a layabout or an idiot with nothing you can get to grips with.'

6

The morning dozed in the grass although the clear light had driven away all shadows when the girl woke up. The light seemed to be brought to the farm from all directions, from a hidden glow in space and not from the sun.

Somehow the girl felt herself threatened by this great blinding light and she looked forward to going into the warm twilight of the cowshed. For an instant a comfortably calm blindness struck her eyes when she entered the dusk there which was buzzing with the heavy, moist breathing of clumsy animals. Until now she preferred to associate with them than with people. Their curiosity, their nuzzling with moist chops, was even more human than the humans' dry encroachments and prying. The cows gave heavy snorts after first thrusting their wet chops at her and then their reddish-white tongues into their nostrils, as if to taste her smell. 'I wish I could live in a huge cow,' she thought. It was only the smell that made her shy from them slightly. It reminded her of dirty underwear.

The moment she entered the cowshed, she sensed that something peculiar was going on, but could see nothing. She untied the cows in the front stall, half blinded at the border between dusk and light by the door, and they plodded out clicking their hoofs which were all too small to be able to support their heavy bodies. When she went up to the most eccentric cow, which never stayed in a group with the others, she saw to her astonishment that out of its backside stood a moist head with closed eyes, covered in goo. For an instant she imagined that a spell had been cast on the cow during the night, making it two-headed, and the head at its rear was dead. She had heard countless stories about cows that change shape, both on the radio and at her home, and had even read about them in children's books and heard people talking about them during her short stay on the farm. Perhaps it was the constant metamorphosis of humans and animals that made her notice immediately that reality was not to be taken for granted in the countryside. She looked for a while at the sticky, dead head. The cow calmly turned its front head along its side to see how the rear head was getting on. It was astonished about the head's death and was doubtless afraid, because so much of the whites of its eyes were showing; in fact it could hardly believe its own eyes and mooed at the head to bring it back to life. Afterwards it looked at the girl for help. Then she saw that the backside head yawned peculiarly or tried to moo, but only a low noise could be heard. The head at the rear was much smaller than the head at the front and almost bald beneath the slime.

The girl stared dumbfounded at the two-headed cow. At the same time she realized that it had been a peculiar night and the light was on the mysterious side that morning.

Without further thought she ran out to fetch the farmer. He hurried to the scene, immediately grabbed the side of the rear head's mouth with both hands, pushed the cow hard with his right foot and braced himself in the dung with his left one. Then he strained mightily and went red in the face around his mouth and eyes.

Under such strain the cow looked along its side once again with a completely helpless expression on its face. When it saw the farmer's actions it snorted. Then it curled its tongue into a loop and licked itself lovingly as if the commotion around its backside were none of its business. It belched disdainfully, snorted at the air and shook its head. Then the farmhand took hold of the farmer's hands in the jaws of the head too, and they tugged.

'Hold me round the waist and pull me too, girl. That's right, that's right,' he said with a laugh.

She obeyed at once. At that very instant they toppled straight over backwards, almost squashing her, and the next thing she knew was that the farmer was holding a scrawny calf in his arms and the cow was mooing and rushed stiffly to its feet with a great cracking of joints and clattering of hoofs.

'Your cows are so in-bred they can't even be bothered to stand up to give birth,' said the farmhand.

The calf and its limbs sprang straight to life. It staggered slightly, in fact, but the cow welcomed it, licked its body, cleaned it thoroughly with its tongue and ate, but ignored the gunge that hung out of its backside.

'Yep,' said the farmer to the girl. 'Enchanted cows with two heads are a very strange thing.'

'So are women too when they're in that state,' added the farmhand, smiling at her.

'They certainly are,' she answered in a grown-up voice and tried to joke around for the first time in the same way as country people.

Afterwards she made a grumbling sound, gave a furtive glance sideways and then slightly up into the air, as if she were looking to see what the weather was like inside the cowshed. Country people were always looking to see what the weather was like, even though they kept a careful watch on the weather reports. They even looked up at the ceiling while pausing for thought in the middle of conversation at the dinner table. She even tried to make herself a little boorish, grinned as if she had discovered the secret of life that morning through her company with the animals.

The farmhand had sometimes tried to teach her this kind of braggadocio and said solemnly, 'My girl, if you want to cut a figure among the people here, light a match in public, put it behind you and fart on the flame.'

He showed her how to. She noticed that the flame flared slightly. When he made her sniff him afterwards, she could not smell anything. Then he said, 'Just you wait, my girl.'

She waited calmly. After a while he lifted his leg once more, let rip and asked, 'Can you smell anything now?'

She pondered without saying a word, but answered with her expression, 'Somewhat more than somewhat.'

'Farmers still keep this bodily lore alive,' he said. 'But you must never show these noble arts in barns or at petrol stations. They are popular at country dances when young men begin to feel tipsy; but

30

girls must never charm boys with this until the boys are sloshed. Remember that.'

On saying this he made her promise solemnly always to chew a coffee bean when she was old enough to have a partner, get married and get drunk from sheer boredom at all her consumer comforts.

'Then your husband will never smell alcohol on your breath even if you've been paralytic in the kitchen all day,' he said.

She promised solemnly always to chew coffee beans if she got drunk and wanted to conceal it from her husband.

'Don't your parents teach you these survival skills?' he asked in surprise.

'No,' she replied.

'Children don't get any upbringing in towns and cities any more,' he said. 'You'll end up getting experienced from your stay here this summer. You'll be a true woman by the autumn.'

She could tell somehow that he was telling the truth.

'What if I don't smoke?' she asked.

'Then you'll have to go around with a chewed matchstick in your mouth, of course,' he answered. 'But chewing matches suits men better than women. Toothpicks are smarter and suit women. He's always chewing a matchstick but she chews a toothpick; that's a suitable arrangement for a happy couple. Anyway, it's mainly boys who do those tricks at dances. Girls go completely mad about them then, especially boys who chew matchsticks in the right side of their mouths so that their wisdom teeth show. But you must never ever let your husband chew the sulphur on it, otherwise he'll lose his urge completely.'

So she solemnly promised the farmhand never to let her husband chew the sulphur and he promised to teach her as the summer progressed not only the ways of man but the ways of man and wife too.

'The ways of man and wife are not always compatible in daily life,' he said.

'Of course not,' she said, and bowed her head because the farmer's wife had reprimanded her by saying, 'It's not proper Icelandic to say "sure" when you answer or agree with something.

31

'Because we are not sure about anything in life even though we are a clever nation descended from the kings of Norway. The right thing to say is "of course".'

'Kings, to say nothing of queens, always say "of course",' the farmhand had said too.

The girl had untied all the cows from their stalls. While she was driving them to the meadow and watching the eccentric cow and its calf she pondered what the farmer's wife had said and the farmhand too, and whether she herself were perhaps a princess under a spell watching the dung-covered tails of the cows, far as it was below her dignity.

When she noticed that the cow's udder had different teats from the day before, she thought of what the farmhand had shown her once behind the cowshed. After that she regarded cows' udders as huge male balloons with countless little teats.

'Men have one teat on their udders,' he had told her in concealment and in confidence.

At the back of cows' udders were dwarf teats, like the one the farmhand had shown her of his own. But that had grown suddenly when it was being milked and she watched it for a long time, until it spurted out several jets of what he called 'men's milk'. Afterwards it went limp like the cow's teats had done before, but now they were all as stiff as the farmhand's single teat had been.

That evening she watched how much milk spurted out of the cow's front teats, when the farmer's wife squeezed them while saying that she always milked cows by hand when they had just given birth.

Some time in the night the girl heard a slight rumpus and creaking in the bedroom where the farmer and his wife slept. Her broken sleep merged with what they had eaten after dinner, which the farmer and the farmhand called 'whey'. When they stood up from table, the farmhand whispered to her, 'Keep your wits about you but pretend you're snoring contentedly, and you'll hear some quiet creaking coming from their bedroom.'

For a long time she tried to stay awake but eventually she thought she would die of drowsiness listening to the way the farmhand puffed away calmly in his sleep. In her broken sleep she saw him suddenly stretch out his naked arm into the dusky air and keep it up there for quite a long time while he slept, then finally he slipped it back under his quilt and went on puffing.

A queasy feeling went through her stomach as she watched the arm rise mysteriously and without reason up into the air then arch slightly towards the window which had been covered with a white curtain.

There's no doubt it's all true and correct that the farmhand said, the thought occurred to her. She had noticed herself that she felt strange inside after eating the whey. And doubtless everyone turned strange, not just her who had never before eaten that white jelly which was boiled in a little pot inside a bigger pot with boiling water in it, and the smaller one danced in the bubbling, boiling water and gave off strange noises when it tapped against the side of the big pot, until the milk turned into a stiff jelly.

She did not understand this and thought, 'I'm a problem child; I'm nine years old and I've been sent to the countryside.'

7

Her mother wrote letters to her regularly, every fortnight, generally about how healthy it was for her body and mind to stay in the countryside until autumn. She said she could tell from her letters how quickly she had grown up and learned lots of manners – 'and now you'll never do anything naughty ever again'.

Just before she ended the letter with 'All the best, Yours, Mother' she somehow began to ramble, probably feeling obliged to soar a little to show how genuine her emotions were and how much maternal love was contained in her words. For this reason she mixed them with the word of God. She only did that in letters. She also told her that the country people never stole from shops, since they cultivated the land and their souls at the same time, just as they did the fields, so that the innocent lambs would have hay to eat in the winter: 'The sweet-scented angelica-green hay from the meadows in our souls: all the teachers and vicars say this is integrity and healthy thought for our nation.'

Then she told her how everyone knew that a mixture of sea air and country air was by far the healthiest air in Iceland, the health books said so. 'There are two vitamins from the lap of nature that God has mixed and can be used to improve weaknesses in little girls and their behaviour. Here there is no countryside outside town, just heathland, and that must be what turns people into thieves. Everyone robs everyone else.

'Dear daughter, you have been apprehended twice for having stolen sandwiches from eight shops, but without going out into the street with your booty, you were caught in the act, you were found gobbling them down behind the shelves. As if you never get a bite to eat from your father and me . . . Did you polish everything off from those empty marmalade jars that were found under the shelves too? I think it's bad enough stealing sandwiches without you going off straight afterwards to eat your booty in secret, right in front of the customers. My darling, proper thieves never do that. You just set a bad example. What would happen if people just stormed into shops when they were hungry, grabbed sandwiches from the fridge and opened the tins on the spot, because you don't need tin openers any more, and gorged themselves secretly between the shelves, then left with innocent expressions and didn't buy anything? . . . You ought to live in harmony with nature in the countryside – that's the great demand which is made of everybody these days – and uproot from within you, with God, all that is evil in your own bad nature.

'I wish and ask you all this, your dear and loving mother,' she wrote at the end.

Afterwards her father added a few sentences about how he could tell from her letters that she was growing up, 'you're writing pretty well,' and he could read between the lines that she was filling out. 'You'll surely have breasts and hips like a true woman when you come home. Eat a lot,' he said, and finished the letter with a sentence that the vicar had said when he was confirmed: '"Be true right until death and I shall give you the crown of life." I've always felt like I've got a crown on my bonce after that. Your dear father.'

The days went by and she could tell for herself how she was filling out everywhere. She was spread so wide so hollow inside that she could easily slip out of herself, the little girl, to resemble the farmer's wife in her speech and the farmhand in her thoughts. When she did so, it was as if water were flowing out of her soul and merging with the landscape.

She let the strange water that filled her flow easily into the cows and the flowers, the marshland and the mountain in the distance. It was a slightly melancholy flow, but it brought comfort to be able to swim on her own or fly in it whenever she wanted, against the rain yet in the same manner as it, up into the blue evening sky.

Sometimes when she had the weekend free, if she was lying idly in the sand by the river and listening to the ceaseless lapping of the grey current of the water, she could feel how her thoughts turned into a clear flood that rushed to face the sky, but at the same time another flood would break, both similar and dissimilar, which flowed like dirty water out of her legs and into the river.

What ruined her happiness at such moments was how many girls had fathers who owned grocer's shops. At the same time she did not want to become like the country people and own the same things as they did: meadows, horses, jeeps and farm animals. Above all she longed to get away, but could not even return home in her mind, because the mountain cast a shadow on the route. Only in the evenings could she manage with her feelings to flap her arms and see herself take to the air in a bright glow. But she never made it home, but plunged instead and crashed on to the mountain like a black fly. Then she would give a start and pant for breath, but could still fall back asleep, even though she thought she would never sleep another wink after that terrifyingly vertiginous dream and the frightful drop into the mountain lake.

'The day that I go off on horseback to the foot of the mountain with the other children, I shall climb it and fly off the edge,' she thought feebly as she dozed.

One time she was in the marshland by the peat ditches, which she had been warned against approaching, but went to the edge of one and looked down into the black water. Then she noticed that there were busy bugs there, swimming quickly either up through the surface or down into the invisible depths. They waded the water with their legs in a strange, swift and intense game. They also seemed able to walk on the ground, and perhaps fly. These versatile talents seemed to instil them with uncontrollable delight. The game was not only a game of a certain *joie de vivre*, but also served a specific function: the bugs fetched little white bubbles from the surface, hung them on their backsides and darted down with them into the black depths.

Perhaps they are in the service of some monster lying hidden in the ditch, and they're fetching air so it can breathe. It doesn't dare to come up out of the darkness itself and into the light of day, the brightness would kill it. Monsters can't stand sunlight. That's why the bugs are busying themselves so with fetching air for her lungs.

This was what she thought, even though she knew quite well that it was probably fantasy and nonsense.

If I fell into the ditch I would die, because I could never make it to the high bank by my own strength and unaided, because the ditch isn't full right up to the bank. I wouldn't be able to reach up with my hands. I couldn't pull myself up back on to the edge. The sun would shine as it is today, I'd be alone and no one would see me. No one would hear me even if I kept myself afloat by swimming and shouted with my head up out of the water, drained by exhaustion and the cold. How long could I keep myself afloat? Above me would be the clear sky, blue air and peaceful, beautiful flowers growing on the banks. I would hear the endless sweet song of the birds while I was struggling not to lose my strength as I swam, in the hope that someone would come and help me. The cows might be passing by, come up to the bank, look down, snort, shit and have a drink, and the dogs, lambs and sheep would do the same, because they are thirsty and contented in the good weather. But they wouldn't do anything to help me, except perhaps low, bleat or bark into the air. The waterbeetles would continue their frenzied swimming to take air to the monster, otherwise it would suffocate and stop giving them orders, and then they wouldn't know what they were supposed to do and would die confused and helpless in the depths too. But they wouldn't do a thing for me while I was on the verge of giving up and suffocating and drowning. Then gradually I would hear a buzzing in my ears and see everything in a haze, feel the water inside me . . . and then disappear into it . . .

She stood near to the edge of the ditch and moved closer while she let her mind wander, moved nearer to it the longer she thought in a cold trance that aroused rejoicing within her breast. Nothing was as wonderful as thinking about death on a fine day, a Sunday afternoon in the countryside when you have the day off and nothing to do in the midst of the birdsong and scent of moist earth which is covered with swollen flowers and plants. The sweetest thing then is to imagine your own death in a peat ditch while nature is shrouded with the tranquillity of the afternoon and you are full of the vigour of youth, an endless distance away from your imaginings, young and in the bloom of life.

Now she was standing on the brink. She could go no farther without falling and had her toes over the edge and could clearly see her own reflection on the still surface of the water.

'Dive in, dare to die,' she told herself in a whisper and could feel the water closing around her, cold and luxurious, because everything was over.

Her body dissolved and vanished into the blue. The presence of death made her confused, as if she were in another world.

'Now it's only less than one step between life and death,' she thought. 'Oh, take it. Go on, step out once and for all and jump into the ditch.'

The flies buzzed. The breeze filled the air with the scent of flowers and doubtless the birds were singing with their chirping about how transitory but wonderful life is.

'Should I take the step?' she asked, lifted her foot, stretched it out and saw the worn sole of her shoe reflected in the water.

The knowledge on the brink of the peat ditch about the tiny distance between life and death paralysed her and she suddenly lay down exhausted on the ground. It was so easy to stop having any other future, no other than the momentary one, the instant it would take her to walk half a step with one foot over the bank to meet her end in the water. Death is so peculiarly close to life. It follows it close behind, it is born with it. Sometimes it guides your whole life. And you can walk out of life and into death, but there's no way to turn back to life except once: only when you're born.

On realizing this she felt the heat from tears in her eyes, without crying. The universe soared towards her. The air pressed her down against the earth which itself could not press her to it of its own will. She just lay exhausted in the grass and felt how the earth embraced her in her mind, because she made it do that. Really you have to do everything yourself, she sensed. There is no great and truer friend than yourself. In their minds, all people have to make themselves ready-made arms from whatever material is at hand at any time and they chance upon, if they want to enjoy being embraced by the one they yearn for.

She rocked from side to side. She felt safe on the bank of the ditch, lifted one leg and watched it reflected in the water.

'You're safest if you lie down,' she thought. 'You can't fall when you're lying down.'

Down in the deep ditch lived the monster that she imagined to herself and was constantly sending its black servants swimming swiftly to fetch air bubbles so that it could go on breathing and giving them orders . . . so that they were able to obey blindly, and the monster to breath in the place where no one could see it . . .

8

When haymaking time drew near, the farmer's daughter came home unannounced in a little red car. Life in the household changed at once. Everyone grew somehow happy, not only the people but also the farm animals, nature and the guests. Even the weather seemed to improve; it stayed dry for many days. The daughter had brought happiness with her, but didn't occupy herself with anything in particular to begin with.

'I'm infinitely tired in all spheres,' she said.

The sun shone, and one day she stopped lying around, and fetched her old bicycle from the shed and cycled to the other farms to celebrate her return with her neighbours. She did not say in so many words, but rather indirectly with her attitude and expression, 'There's nothing better than being at home with your parents during the summer holidays.'

She appeared to enjoy it. If she did not spend the following days cycling to other farms or along the pavement around the house, or going even farther into the countryside in her red car, she would saddle her horse and ride off into the beyond. In the evenings and at weekends she went on long riding trips with her father. They both owned pedigree horses. She rode by his side, they smiled occasionally at each other and her hair and the horse's mane rippled in the wind. The father rode wearing an old but appropriate check tweed peaked cap which he tipped to the right and thereby turned himself into a handsome middle-aged man who clearly kept himself in good shape, was still full of life, so that it could be imagined that here was an eligible male who combined vestiges of youth with full maturity and physical and mental experience of life, but preferred the company of women to marriage with one, and was riding along with his latest fiancée and not his daughter.

When he dismounted and took off his cap, this exotic respectable air vanished and he turned back into an ordinary farmer.

The girl had never before known this delight that everyone seemed to share. The effect of joy on her, on the other hand, was that she pushed her mind out into a twilight where her moods became strange and she tried to be alone, because she knew only the joy of the particular, which you share with yourself or no one at all and which produces on your face a static, mysterious smile the cause of which no one can tell. It is introverted and conceals itself all the more by alighting sadly on to lips which back off slightly to hide away in the mouth.

Booming laughter resounded around the house. At the dinner table in the evenings there was joking and endless stories were told about people, with an underlying note of malice. These were uneventful but hurtful stories about people from other farms. The daughter came back bestowing them after her constant cycle trips. She seemed to set off for the nearby farms to fetch back amusing tales about people from the other farms beyond them, but mocked the people who told them. And she played the mouth organ too. Noticing that merriment had the opposite effect on the girl, the daughter stroked her hair mockingly and said, 'Little grumpy, you've brought a bit of that rotting smell from the sea with you in your soul.'

But she took her words back at once and added, in an unnaturally gentle tone of voice, 'Of course I don't mean it – or do I? You mean everything you say instinctively.'

The girl's thoughts could not swing endlessly back and forth according to the sound of stories about people she did not know. And she did not understand insinuation or when the daughter promised to let her sit in front while she rode her bike, if she did something or other that she was going to ask her to do in private, but then she would change her mind suddenly, as soon as she could see that her curiosity was aroused. 'No, on second thoughts, I won't . . . sorry . . .' she said apologetically.

She laughed and sang and everyone welcomed her at first, but after a short while her merriment had become so demanding and merciless towards people who could not keep up with her with their laughter, that after a week many of them had begun to flee from her *joie de vivre* or tried to ignore it. Visitors largely stopped calling. Then the girl started laughing the loudest of them all, and if she came anywhere near the daughter she would put on a smile immediately, ready to laugh at her jokes.

'You've grown so jolly I can hear you'll turn out to be a farmer's wife,' the farmer said one evening at the dinner table. 'Life in the countryside has made you free.'

She let out a roar of laughter in agreement. The farmer became flustered and, not knowing how to react to her exaggerated behaviour, swung out at her, but missed. After that he was half gloomy for a while and constantly on his guard. He looked at her enquiringly with an expression that implied that nothing could ever be understood completely, you just have to believe that you understand. His enquiring look, especially if they ran into each other where no one else could see them, aroused a feeling of guilt within her and she stopped laughing, so that she would not be given a blow or a story about herself, because everyone knew why she was there. 'If I don't laugh at gossip about strangers and never tell stories about other people, then they'll keep quiet about me, and I won't get stories told about me here, even if I have done something worth telling back home,' she thought vaguely.

For a few days the girl longed to admit to the others that she was just pretending, that her laughter was fake, she couldn't care less about anything except one thing which she would never tell anyone. The longing to confess was so strong that she had to repress it with a toughness she had never felt before and did not know herself capable of. Then she decided to struggle on in silence until the autumn, but with certain roars of laughter in the wrong places.

Once when she laughed instinctively without knowing why, the farmer's wife gave her a slap around the face that echoed for a long while within her, but she said nothing even though her face was stinging and she was on the verge of tears, and went back to her work instead. After this she gradually reduced her laughter so that no one would notice, until she stopped it completely. The daughter soon noticed the change and said, 'Now you've got the old rotten fish back inside you.'

'Stop it,' said her mother.

From this point on the girl managed to be reasonably jolly in company but took her bad moods off by herself. When the others had gone to bed at night, she stayed awake until they were definitely asleep. Then she got up and crept out quietly to watch the mountain which had turned dark in the course of the evening against the light of the sunset. The setting sun made the sky insubstantial, so the mountain became more solid until it broke free from itself and became dark blue in the night. It stopped being a mountain and became just a colour. One morning the farmhand whispered to her, 'It's healthy for girls to sneak out in the nude at night to take a piss on the earth, especially after midnight. I shan't tell you the reason now, you'll find out as soon as you grow up.'

She did not laugh. He looked at her and added, 'When you're young you just do things and don't know why, but then . . .'

'Like what?' she asked.

'Telling lies, pretending things, pretending to have seen or heard something,' he said. 'Some develop a twitch.'

She looked away and felt that he could see right through her.

'Oh, it's all right,' he continued. 'You've still got a long way before you reach old age. The bad things in life don't take over for real until you're more or less old and wise.'

Then he smiled, showed the stumps of his teeth in a grin and spun around, sticking out his hand and pointing his index finger.

'Look at nature all around!' he shouted. 'Oh, this creature of liberty always has its own way and never asks permission for anything from us oppressed but self-satisfied *homo sapiens*.'

Saying this, he bent down suddenly to the girl and stuck his tongue in her mouth. She could taste tobacco on his supple but soft tongue and a painful jab near the bottom of her stomach. He laughed.

'Nature never asks permission to settle down anywhere,' he said. 'Just watch it.'

At his words, she recalled that the dog often snapped at the air for no apparent reason. Cows often mooed without anyone knowing why. The cat miaowed pitifully over and again. Flowers grew in the most unlikely places. What sort of fun could it be for nature if everything's so easy for it? She began to understand that most things grow in defiance of man's will except the grass in the meadow which the farmer had sown, the trees that his wife had planted in rows, the decorative flowers and vegetables. Some of the most beautiful flowers grew in the midst of unremarkable scrap iron, oil slicks or in the rubbish, and she visualized a half-erased image of a flower on a rock outcrop, slumbering in the wind from the sea. The nakedness of the outcrop and the sky forced its way into her fuzzy mind and swept away the plants, the animals and the laughter of the people making hay which was drying to the whirring of machines.

'It's difficult to live,' said the farmhand and grinned. 'But you can be sure, you'll manage to get older with the help of the years. You can do anything with them. Without trying.'

For some while he stuck his tongue in her mouth every time they met on their own and he said, 'I do that just because. You're still a child, but when you're older the memory of my tongue in your mouth will incite you with painful yearning in your lovelessness.' He laughed and gave her a wry look. 'Then you will only have the memory of this tongue, nothing but that even if you are married and even if you have had children and been unfaithful and resorted to having children with your husband just before you get old and past it, simply to save your marriage: not from love, not from anything apart from a hopeless rescue measure.'

Then he bent back down to her and added, 'Bite my tongue when you feel it; but only once, on the tip.'

She did so, a little perplexed, and suddenly he started crying and ordered her to go. After that he stopped playing this game and for a while he pretended not to notice her.

9

All of a sudden the daughter changed completely and for a while she could not be made to say a word; then she turned obstreperous and even spiteful. After that she started talking in long spurts and her parents looked furtively out of the corner of their eyes at her and dumbfounded at each other.

Now she had stopped gallivanting around in the car or on her bike and had become excessively energetic about work, generally someone else's rather than her own, and wanted to change everything. She was industrious in the kitchen. No one could get a look in anywhere for her busybodying. Either she had just done the job or was about to do it, or she would say peevishly that it was unnecessary. In the evenings she sat in the sitting room, devotedly knitting or sewing. If anyone turned up she would talk to him as if addressing all mankind rather than an individual.

At the dinner table she hardly talked of anything except their home computer and the foddering of cows with the assistance of a hay-feed program which her friend and classmate was writing on a farm at the foot of the mountain. She claimed that at long last the world was heading for a new, completely unknown and certain remarkable future.

'This is the first time in history that the future deserves the name future,' she said.

Her father listened with interest, but clearly for something other than the meaning of her words or their prophetic value. Sometimes he said in a fluster, 'Take it easy, come on, take it easy!'

'Since the computer was unknown until recent decades, our future on earth has been a random version of the past and uneven recyclings of it. But mankind's future will not be determined by any program,' she said with a cold collectedness. 'Mankind is heading for the first time in history beyond the solar system, beyond earthly laws, beyond natural genetics towards beautiful, real, enhanced genetics and into cosmic experience.'

Her mother shrugged and said comfortingly, 'Just try to eat something. That's always turned out to be the best thing for us, whatever science says.'

'I reckon that with computer-controlled foddering, you'll be able to milk three times a day,' she said. 'Why are cows only milked twice a day, mornings and evenings?'

'It's the custom,' her father said unenthusiastically.

'Away with tradition,' said the daughter and started lashing out at the milking machine that was put on the cows' teats. Instead of letting them out into the meadow, she wanted to have them permanently on-line to it in the cowshed, to send the milk into storage the moment it was secreted into their udders.

'You'll ruin my cows,' her father said unenthusiastically.

Then she lashed out at the hay, because the weather was dry every day. Whatever she took on, she said, she was a match for three grown men.

The farmhand kept his eyes fixed on her or looked at her askance, grinning and pretending to be rendered helpless by how hard she worked.

'When do we get to benefit from computer-controlled women?' he asked.

'You never will,' she answered curtly.

'Why not?'

'In the cybernetic world I will get to benefit from myself for the first time, mate,' she answered at once.

The daughter was all over the place, dressed in blue trousers, and everything became light work in her hands: the haymaking machines, sewing needles, pots and the people on the farm. She ran the home. Once she showed the girl her hands and said, 'I'm ambidextrous.'

Her hands looked like little, neat spades.

'How do you mean?' asked the girl.

'I'm left-handed and right-handed too.'

She seemed to prefer spending the day on the tractor, in between running to the harvester, tedder or jeep. What was more, she clearly began to swell with vigour, until there was no concealing that it was not her stomach muscles but that her condition was beginning to show. After that her stomach stood out like a lump in her trousers, which were half unbuttoned at the belt with the flies invariably open, so that her brownish belly and little white knickers could be seen in a bundle at the end of her groin.

Then she started telling the future, laying cards in the evening at dinner, in between pushing her heavy and always newly washed hair up from her forehead with a slow movement, sweeping it back on to the nape of her neck and flicking it over to her right shoulder, at the same time as she urged everyone to go on a computer-training course, turned pensive while holding a card in the air, laid it over another card and advocated the need for women to have children out of wedlock, they shouldn't regard men as anything except in the form of frozen sperm for fertilization.

When she was in this mood her mother became uneasy but her father withstood the cold joking and garrulousness by making himself look expressionless and letting his facial muscles go slack.

'If the sperm can stand being frozen, the woman's child will be healthy,' she said, with a snort at men.

This gave her the opportunity to refer quite frequently to the father of the expected baby in her womb, but she implored them not to ask who he was.

'He's nothing and I don't want to hear his name,' she said emphatically. 'I own my child myself.'

Her mother tried to calm her.

'Of course,' she said. 'But don't over-exert yourself on the machinery. Everyone can overdo things.'

'Do you reckon she'll over-exert herself, a healthy country lass?' said the farmer.

The daughter did not listen to them, but said, in a lofty tone with a glassy glint in her eyes, that the father of her child was dead, at least in her eyes.

'To me he's more than dead, less than nothing,' she added. 'He has never existed in any form except as something small, maybe a little midwinter frolic and then something dead and buried.'

All the same, they thought they could tell that he lived on the farm at the foot of the mountain which cast its shadow over the direction the girl always looked because she lived far away on the other side of it. The mountain gathered veils of cloud around its head in the evening and the sun turned them red. In this way it seemed to marry the evening, or the evening married it, at each sunset, when they shared their nuptial bed of cloud.

If she was alone with the girl, the daughter would sometimes ask her to come over and put her hand on her stomach. The girl obeyed and could feel the hard belly under the palm of her hand, and a strange sensation passed through her, as if she were not touching a woman's stomach, but rather a strange, big ball or globe.

'Of course, you thought pregnant women's stomachs were soft,' she said. 'Didn't your mother ever let you put your hand on her globe before she brought your sister into the world?'

'No,' answered the girl. 'It's rude touching pregnant stomachs.'

The daughter roared with laughter.

'What isn't rude then!'

The girl bowed her head at being laughed at. She felt nauseous, and in her mind she thrust her hands deep inside the stomach, where she groped around for a while in the dark, found the child which was lying there hunched up, and strangled it. At the same moment her own mother appeared, stooped over something inside her head. She had her back turned to her. The girl took hold of her shoulders and laid her down backwards. Then she saw that her palms were glued to the huge stomach. She rolled her mother over, sending her tumbling down a slope like a jar with two ears, and she bumped into a rock and shattered. The girl was startled, started to cry and ran off.

'You're a weirdo,' the daughter called out in a loud voice. 'You're a real case!'

One night the girl dreamed that the daughter had disappeared. Seized by terror, she woke up, got out of bed and crept out. She looked for her in the cowshed and eventually found her lying in a stall, two-headed on all fours. The head sticking out of her backside was crying furiously. When it saw the girl it began to moo and foam bubbled out of the corners of its mouth. She was going to use the same technique as the farmer, lock her fingers inside its mouth, grip the jaw, press her foot against the arse bone and pull the extra head out, when the daughter suddenly got up, roared with laughter, pulled a scornful face at her and said, 'You'll never be a proper woman if you let yourself be tricked like that in a dream.'

The girl woke up for real, but wisps of dreams still roamed around in her mind and wrapped around her, pulling her towards them and concealing her in the soft grey folds of some kind of garment. There she re-encountered the daughter, who once again asked her to put her palm on her bloated stomach. The girl obeyed and the stomach breathed rapidly. Then she did on purpose what she had done unconsciously in her mind: she plunged both hands mercilessly into it, as if the stomach were a huge egg with a flimsy shell, and she looked down to see whether the yolk and the white weren't oozing out. The daughter laughed out loud. The girl was seized with terror. She tried to snatch her hands back, but they had stuck tight to the belly.

'You'll never get rid of me after this,' said the daughter, shrieking and bending over her, her face disfigured by laughter and howling at the same time.

The girl woke with a start and saw the anguished calm of night around her. She could hear the howling in the visible calm, either in her sleep or in the waking state. There was a bluish light in the bedroom and she knew it was a summer night. The howling was carried in from somewhere and seemed to slip out from a secret room inside the sleep of wakefulness. Then she slowly got up and followed the noise, as if creeping along a thread in her breast.

When she stepped out of bed she saw that the farmhand was lying awake but motionless and was clearly also listening to the screams, which were not exactly audible to the ear. Inside the room all the objects and the brightness of night too were more unrealistic than in a dream setting. The light night was a kind of dream of long days which never fade out entirely and are therefore never lost in nocturnal darkness, but glow like fluorescent lamps in the night.

The farmhand had probably been aware of the girl. He rolled on to one side and looked over towards her, with a neutral and vacant look in his eyes which stayed wide open and awake in his sleep. Someone was laughing and crying at the same time in the far distance. Gradually the girl realized and thought that it was the birds and the murmuring of the river in the night, but then a finger of light gripped her mind and she was wide awake: it was the farmer's daughter laughing and crying outside the house. There was the sound of a car. The girl was about to rush to the window to see what was happening when the farmhand suddenly thrust out his arm from beneath the quilt in his sleep, blocking her way, and he grabbed her leg so that she almost slammed down on his bed with her hands stretched out towards the window.

The blue of night grew richer as he pulled her into bed with him. He placed her up against his body and she could feel a peace passing through her which she had never experienced before. She wanted to die and be buried in his dreams.

'No,' he said in his sleep, and nothing else.

The girl could smell the farmhand's scent, the scent of his body, sleep and underwear. It was the scent of an adult male and of physical labour. While he watched her, gaping, the scent from him increased. Again she was seized by a longing to die and be buried in his dream.

'It's just rueful love,' he said, and released her.

Instead of going to the window, she went sheepishly back to her bed, looking at him constantly over her shoulder on her way across the floor. He stretched out his arm in the direction of nothing in particular, and she watched him, the way his fingers gripped because the back of his hand was turned downwards. She also watched him from her bed, the way he clenched his fist into the air several times without looking towards her. Then he put his hand on his forehead and covered it, and both eyes, beneath his palm.

The girl thought she would never get to sleep, but she fell fast asleep before she knew it.

The next morning the daughter was nowhere to be seen. She had left. No one said anything, any more than if she had never been there or had never existed. There was no mention of her. But the house was emptier than before. Every object, both indoors and outside, gradually returned to its place and no one moved any of them unless it was necessary. The old routine went on. The farmhand looked after the cowshed and milking the cows. They all did their appointed jobs. When the girl came to drive out the cattle she asked him, 'What was it?'

The farmhand looked towards her and asked, 'What was what?'

Then he looked at her boorishly and answered, 'Me. It was me.'

10

Only a little more than a week passed and the daughter returned, slim, silent, rid of her stomach but with no child in her arms. Shortly afterwards she sank into languor. Her mother had gone somewhere in the jeep to fetch her. When they got out of it in front of the house she tried to be noisy and impressive. It was if all the former wind and energy had entered her from her daughter, who gave the occasional shrug with an expression on her face that suggested the world was none of her business any more. On the way into the house she noticed the tedder and rushed straight over to it. Her mother ignored it.

It was early in the morning during dry weather when the hay had been left spread out through the night. The mother went into the kitchen to cook a leg of veal. The farmer had slaughtered a calf early in the morning, with the help of the farmhand. The girl had not driven it out with the cows. The leg of veal belonged to the calf she had seen sticking out from the cow's backside. It was almost a month old and the cow had stopped sniffing around it and sticking its tongue up its tail to see if that was the calf or if it had changed suddenly into another calf not her own. Perhaps the cow had forgotten it. But when it was missing from herd that morning the cow went berserk, refused to obey, tore itself away from the rest and jogged, mooing, over the field. The girl repeatedly tried to drive the cow into the pasture, but it turned back, snorted with its eyes popping and let out prolonged moos.

For all that the cow charged around the side of the field like this, the calf did not answer, it lay slain, skinned and with its head by its tail on top of a newspaper, its severed neck exposed to the sun. The body had been chopped into pieces. The cow roamed in circles around the field, a clumsy animal running so that its udder slopped about. It mooed and splashed its sides with water and mud from the marsh, slightly resembling a growling dog. Its lowing was short and tearful. It charged around like this for most of the day, in between grazing to gather energy anew and rest, but it became increasingly clumsy as evening approached, because its udder, swollen with milk, could hardly fit between its legs. The udder looked set to rip and send the white milk spurting out of the teats. The cow was looking for its calf and even attacked the gate, rubbed the crown of its head against it and butted it. When the fencing did not give way the cow rose ponderously to its rear legs and banged its front hoofs against the lower strut. The girl watched it, astonished that this clumsy, easy-going animal should be capable of and preserve such tragedy within itself that it moved in spasms and foamed at the mouth.

Children had come over from the other farms that morning to watch the slaughter. These were country children who enjoyed watching animals being slaughtered. The calf had stood by itself on the field for a little while, in sunlight so bright that it seemed to shine out of a newly born world in the cloudless day. The children jostled to put their arms round its neck, pushing each other out of the way, scuffled to get up close to the animal which was waiting calmly and slightly absent-mindedly among the grass and a few buttercups and dandelions. The girl put her arm around its neck, too. Her face could feel heavy breathing, but the calf stood still as the grave and did not even swish its tail.

'Now you are supposed to die and will not exist in ten minutes' time, just imagine it,' she whispered in its ear. 'Do you know how little time you have left?'

The calf gave a tiny snort.

The children kissed it on the forehead. They patted it and looked straight into the dark, shiny eyes which it hardly blinked in the sunshine, alone and far away from its mother and all others, from the children's embraces too, calm in the sunshine, face to face with death.

When the children heard what the girl said they were amused and formed a laughing queue so that they all could whisper in its ear, 'You're supposed to die and stop existing. Do you know that?'

The farmhand had sharpened the knives and laid them, polished and honed, side by side, on a canvas sack which was fawn-coloured like the calf. The blades did not glitter in the sunshine, these were old and tarnished knives, but still terrifying in the girl's eyes. The farmer ordered the children to clear off round the corner of the house.

'You've said goodbye to the calf gently enough for it to get into heaven,' he said. 'But don't get in the way. You can peep around the corner. We don't want you around here. Come on, take it easy, do what you're told, you can have a bite of him for lunch.'

'He's so nice,' said a boy from the neighbouring farm.

'All right, he'll be even better cooked for lunch if you lot clear off,' answered the farmer, pushing them away. 'My daughter will be here soon and we'll welcome her back with a good feast of veal. All right? You'll join us for lunch. Agreed?'

'Yes,' the children answered in chorus.

Smiling, they disappeared around the corner, but fought for a place to peep out and see how the blood spurted out from beneath the knife.

The girl had gone straight off to round up the cows. No sooner was she out of sight than she turned back, made a rush and hid herself with the others. She too wanted to watch the calf being slaughtered and die. When she came back it was lying on the field, wriggling its legs futilely. The farmhand held it and the farmer cut it with the knife. Her legs went weak too. 'No one can save you now,' she mentally said to the calf. 'You have a minute left to live, half, only a second. Now you'll die.' At the same time she asked it to take a last look at the world. Then the farmer cut its throat and the blood sprayed out in a red jet, moistening the buttercups and flowers, which bowed beneath the splashes but acted as though nothing had happened, covered in blood, shiny yellow and red in the glory of the morning.

The girl put her hand over her mouth and could feel water swirling around her dry eyes. The cups of the buttercups filled up with blood. The sun shone for an instant in an exotic light and mountains seemed absent-minded in the distance, when the calf

54

rolled its eyes and bowed its head. Then the buttercups could no longer hold the blood and drooped towards the earth to empty their cups, but lifted their heads halfway back afterwards.

After the daughter had arrived and sat down on the tedder she immediately saw the cow charging for the fence and mooing. She stopped the engine and called out, 'What's wrong with that old cow?'

No one answered, but the girl was ordered to drive it into the pasture at once. But it came back straight away, mooing loudly. Then the daughter drove the tedder up to the gate and the snorting cow retreated. She screamed at the animal, opened the gate, revved up the engine and drove after it, shooing the cow away, but it came straight back, so she gave up, drove back to the farm and said, 'Have the cows here gone mad too?'

Once again she ordered the girl to drive it into the pasture. She did so, and made a mooing imitation of the calf, but the cow refused to be duped. It did not look at the girl. 'Perhaps it senses that no one can replace anyone else, however much he would like to, because a mourner mourns for something definite that no one can make up for, even if it may be forgotten or vanish from the memory in the course of time,' the girl sensed rather than thought. While her mind fluttered in this way she placed her forehead between the cow's horns, and the cow immediately bowed its head and chops to the ground and snorted into the bedewed grass.

They stood there like that for a while in the sunshine, the girl and the cow in the damp marsh, and in the distance the earth rose up from itself in the *fata Morgana*, as if yearning to seek its celestial essence, but unable to move any farther, or only in another image than that of grey mirages, billowing waves of air at a constant height just above or on the horizon.

Shortly after the girl turned back from driving the cow out for the last time, the farmer's wife called everyone in for lunch. The children from the other farms had returned and had carefully combed their hair to be both clean and tidy when they took part in the feast. They stood bunched together, their hair swept back, smartly dressed, and watched silently how the frenzied flies swarmed on to the remains of

55

the calf, on to the blood which had turned black and dry in the sunshine, and how the buttercups were stuck in the congealed liquid.

When they made their solemn entrance, the house filled up with the aroma of roasted leg of veal. Their mouths started watering and they grew hungry.

The daughter alighted from the tedder and said jokingly, and rather more cheerfully than when she had arrived that morning, 'What's this, a feast? You parents sure know how to celebrate when someone has a foetus aborted just to get her own back when she's been cheated on.'

Her mother hushed at her.

'We cooked the legs for you,' she said then, but was upset. 'Veal is supposed to be rich in blood, so maybe you'll get over it faster.'

'I'll eat and eat,' she said, bent down, stuck her face up at the children and showed them her red-painted claws. 'I'll tear the calf's meat and stuff myself with it, and when I get up from the table I'll have a huge belly again.'

She growled.

The children watched her in admiration, but pretended to be afraid of her claws and the unconvincing grimaces on her face. From their eyes shone gratitude when they chewed the meat and gave secret glances in her direction. It was thanks to her that they had been invited around for a meal and were allowed to eat the delicious veal with her.

While they were sitting eating, the occasional moo could be heard from the cow which had gone back to the fence and was starting to butt against it. The windows were open in the good weather and the aroma of the steak wafted outside. The daughter put down her knife and fork and said brashly, 'Maybe the cow picked up the scent. Don't you reckon she can recognize the aroma of her brazed calf?'

The children started to laugh.

'Are you enjoying eating her calf?' she asked.

'Yes,' they answered with a gasp.

'And how do you think she would moo, kids, if she knew we were in here stuffing ourselves full with it? She'd moo just like this . . .'

The children laughed merrily at her impersonations.

The adults said nothing. The farmer's wife only asked the children not to make their faces too dirty or smear fat on their clothes and not to wipe their fingers on the tablecloth. She got up and tore off a few sheets of kitchen roll and handed them to each of them. She did not go straight back to the table, and spent an exceptionally long time rummaging in the cupboards. The daughter looked over at her, laughed and showed her teeth menacingly. Then she stopped. The girl thought her eyes had gone strange, she was grinning constantly, and she rocked her shoulders every time she put a morsel in her mouth.

'Sweet little moo-moo's calf,' she said, and bared her teeth.

'Great,' the children replied, and fiddled at the meat with their forks, because they were full.

'Have you had enough?' asked the farmer's wife. 'Go out then and don't play with your food. That's a sin.'

The children rushed away from the table and outdoors. Suddenly they pelted for the gate to see the cow. One of them said, 'We've just wolfed down your calf.'

The cow snorted.

Afterwards they gave it a tragic look, but the cow did not seem to understand anything.

They leapt back to the house and went indoors, to let the daughter know they had spoken to the cow, told it they had eaten its calf, and it didn't give a damn.

'Tut,' said the farmer's wife, and told her daughter to go and rest after the meal. 'You're still frail.'

'Oh, Mum, really . . .' the daughter answered impatiently. 'I belong to the modern generation and I don't need any rest.'

The girl strolled on her own down to the gate to see the cow, which was standing beside it, lifting its head and mooing at the farm. The daughter was on the haymaker and drove up to the girl, who asked, 'Does it know we're digesting the calf in our stomachs?'

Then the other children came rushing over. They had heard the question and started panting through their wide-open mouths, right in the face of the cow, which snorted.

'No,' said the daughter. 'Cows don't know anything. That's just cow-acting.'

They looked at the animal for a while, and then she added, 'Oh, I hate that mooing. Drive it out of here!'

They all drove the cow away together, then sat down on a bank and started picking flowers to put on the grave where they were going to bury the calf's tail and sing beautiful hymns for it, so that they would be praised for being good Christian children.

That evening the cows were driven back to the cowshed past the place where the calf had been slaughtered. Some of them nibbled at the bloody grass. The one that had been its mother and mooed all day did so as well. The buttercups covered with congealed blood disappeared inside them. The girl watched, hardly daring to tread on the spot. Then she did, stepped on it hurriedly with both feet, jumped twice and felt an uncomfortable shudder which wore off into dizziness. She could feel the air erupting inside her and disappearing with a dry whimper out through her mouth. Then she started to vomit and the cows sniffed it, but backed away afterwards from the gushes.

'You've eaten more than you can take, from sheer joy,' said the farmer.

The next morning the cow had completely forgotten the calf and the girl did not feel there was anything mysterious about the patch of ground that had given her the creeps just before milking time the previous evening. It was just as if death had risen up from the black patch of blood, filtered through the soles of her shoes and flowed up through the bottoms of her feet right to her heart, but she had shaken off the feeling in the fine weather, and it would never return to her body now. The patch could largely be distinguished by the fact that there were more flies on it than in other places.

11

The fine weather of those days gradually chopped away at the summer with a gentle apprehension, and the sun made the time pass. The girl hardly paid it any attention during the day. She did not realize time until it started to rain and she heard the drops falling heavily on the pale-green turnip leaves and saw the water forming into pearls and sliding uneasily like quicksilver on the leaves. Time awoke with the light, hollow sound of rain on the leaves which had grown tall and twined almost in a continuous, low roof over the beds of the vegetable patch. But a dry spell came immediately afterwards and the sun made time evaporate anew. On the other hand, eternity awoke in the evenings in the form of loss, after the others were asleep. Because eternity and loss accompany each other. And it is regret which arouses the sense of time, not happiness.

'Yes, if we were always happy there'd be no such thing as time, no clocks, no memories and no diaries either,' said the farmhand one evening as he sat at the table in the room, writing his diary. Then he put his arm around her shoulders.

The farmer had sometimes jokingly mentioned to him that he thought the farmhand preferred the company of letters to that of people. He said this out in the barn and the farmhand admitted it without evasion, but with a slight sense of condemnation.

'I have never been given towards people or animals,' he said. 'All the same, you know that I have fallen in love and I do my job reasonably, because somehow or other you have to live for your emotions and work for your body.'

'If you're telling the truth about the first thing you said, and aren't lying like you usually do,' said the farmer. 'But love isn't enough if you intend to be able to live in the countryside.'

'Really,' said the farmhand. 'I would've thought it was enough everywhere.'

The farmer did not reply, and left.

The girl heard their conversation and felt then that she had gradually learned to love work and treat animals with a feeling that made her more gentle than when she was in the company of people. By now she knew all the horses and knew that the blue dun one she had fetched on her first day was a mare. You could tell an animal's sex straight away if you looked underneath it. She could even tell the horses apart at a great distance. Their names generally depended on the colour of their coats. The same went for cows. She had learned to creep up to the shyest horses and bridle them by beginning to mutter to them in a low voice and enchant them with incomprehensible words and sounds before she reached them, while they looked suspiciously at her out of the corner of their eyes, sensitive and shy. She would approach them quietly then and mentally make herself insubstantial until she could touch their haunches very softly, as if compassion itself were placing its palm upon them. Then she would move without a sound along their sides, with a gentle babbling, pet words, muttering her invented horse language which they listened to attentively and cocked their ears against the breeze, while delicate twitches passed across their skin and the next thing she knew they had opened their mouths and allowed her to conjure the bridle into it.

This was what she found the most peculiar aspect of handling animals, because she did not even understand herself the soothing mutterings that unexpectedly poured out from her, crept out from an unknown place and linked her mind with the horses. Even though she herself did not understand her horse charms, the otherwise wild rather than gentle animals seemed to take them as a confession of love, and sometimes rubbed their heads against her chest, thrust their crowns with white stars on the forehead against the place where her heart was racing with happiness. At this, she evaporated with them in the wet grass of the marshland. A moment later, after she had collected herself, she would stroke the horses on their sensitive lips and feel their hot breathing on her hands and then all over her, the moist current with a pungent scent of chewed grass. Then she would whisper the wondrous language in their ears, and they would move their taut ears back and forth with short, sharp twitches.

If no one could see her, for some reason she would ride the horses with her backside bare, after scratching them behind the ears for a long time.

She was often sent to fetch the daughter's steed when the daughter had one of her frequent bouts of temper and rode off out into the blue to work off her foul mood. The daughter would gallop down to the gate and call out to the girl to open it and hold it while she rode through. Then she would coax the spluttering horse out into the heavy marsh that splashed up in splatters, beating the animal mercilessly with her whip.

Then her father would look up from his work, to watch how she slogged forwards on the dazed horse that had lost control of its gait and felt duly humiliated. If she was in the mood to make the horse plod right through the fen, he would watch her from behind for a long time.

In the evening, when she returned, she would be dark brown and smeared with mud right up to her head. She would walk down the hallway, a brown woman of the earth, laughing menacingly, take a bath, lie in it for a long time as if soaking herself to remove the evil salt from her flesh or soul, and make them keep her dinner waiting interminably for her. Eventually she would go to the table, as if nothing could be more natural, with her hair soaking wet, constantly flicking it back and forth, sending tiny cold needles of water into everyone's faces. On such evenings she had an unusually large appetite.

'Poor thing,' the farmhand said sarcastically to the girl. 'The filly's dropped and now she feels empty inside so she wants something nice to fill her up again.'

He later confided in her that farmhands were always supposed to be in love with the farmer's daughter, but in this case he was an absolute exception.

'And she isn't fond of me either,' he said. 'Not even in secret.'

The girl looked at him behind the cows.

'Love doesn't exist in the countryside any more,' he said. 'The cows are just given an injection. Barns are just to keep the hay in. Nothing exists unless it's for production. That's what people are for too. Love doesn't exist any more.'

None the less, the girl saw that the farmer's wife tried to show affection for her daughter by touching her or patting her, but then she would suddenly sweep the hand away, menacingly, as if to keep her mother at bay with fingers that said, 'Do not touch me.' Then she would add threateningly, if her mother had not understood the body language. 'Mother, I don't need any sympathy, I'm at university now. Don't treat me as if I'm some young maiden who's never learned anything but good Christian behaviour and handicraft from the vicar's wife, or maybe how to play the organ and warble in a shrieking voice those awful Icelandic songs that were ripped off from wishy-washy Danish music in the first place anyway.'

The girl did not know what she meant by such words or behaviour.

After the daughter's speech for the defence, the farmhand said she had said that because she had never read any of the rural novels that were on the bookshelves in her home.

'Just think,' he said. 'There are two big bookcases here full of stories about rural bliss, but the daughter, their only child, hasn't read any of them, just school textbooks, then takes a break from her studies by reading romances and stories about cold-hearted, free-living lawbreakers. And then the countryside is left alone and abandoned with its past in print, in books on dusty shelves, and no one wants to learn about it.'

When the girl looked in the bookcase after that, she felt that she did not want to know anything about life in the countryside either or the bliss that had been there in days gone by. She could not be bothered to make the effort to read speckled books which had brown spines and whose pages gave off a peculiar smell, almost glued together because no one ever opened or browsed through them. They were full of rot, damp and doom which still did not destroy them completely.

The daughter began spending her whole time in the bath to calm down her nerves. She locked herself in the bathroom for hours. If anyone needed to go to the toilet and rattled the door handle, her mother was quick to say, 'She's in the bath.'

Eventually she would come out smelling like an open perfume jar. She had hung a Walkman around her neck and clamped the head-phones over her head with the earpieces plugged in her ears. For a long time she would never go anywhere without wearing her Walkman, not even when she was eating. Her father could not accept her sitting like that, closed to the world, not even listening to the news headlines on the radio or television.

'You ought to keep up with the news,' he said.

'Ooo,' she answered with an indifferent but bored expression. 'For as long as the world goes on there'll be endless battles in Beirut or places like that. And the news features will always be about marvellous machines that have been invented with the specific purpose of saving the world and will doubtless enhance our under-standing of man, but fortunately they always fail as delightfully as ever. Now all the universities are at work on inventing a telepathy device which, it is claimed, will revolutionize computer and electronics development or at least render it obsolete. So there you go, you farmers. The most brilliant scientists say today that the telepathic revolution is certainly just around the corner with all the solutions; you just have to hang on to the problems for a while.'

'Telepathy has been around since the year dot,' said her mother. 'It came with man.'

'Everything's been around since the year dot, Mother, but you still have to invent it,' the daughter replied in an idiotically gentle tone. 'The problem is making it visible and concrete. And telepathic messages have never been sent among us humans on a scientific basis before or by using the most sophisticated hardware, perhaps by satellite, so that all that electronic trash will be obsolete at a stroke before we've even learned to use it properly. At last, they've found the one true button to press that until now has only existed in man's dreams. And all others will become obsolete at the same time.'

'Yours isn't obsolete though, is it?' the farmhand asked out of the blue.

'Well, who knows?' she answered straight back, completely unruffled. 'No, in fact I've got so many buttons that there are plenty in reserve if one gets destroyed. But if science manages to simplify me and exterminate all of them but one, you won't be the one who pushes it and gets me going.'

She said this while giving the farmhand a fixed look, then started giggling.

'I suspect that someone at the University Science Faculty has had a good push on all of your buttons once and for all and you're all buttoned up now and your button-pushing was over and done with in a single winter. You weren't like this last year,' the farmhand said.

The daughter did not answer, but her father lowered his eyes and cleared his throat. The farmer's wife looked at them each in turn as if to ask whether the untouched, dusty rural romances in the bookcase weren't repeating themselves before her very eyes and walking abroad in a new form. Surely these claims and jibes can't be evidence that there really is something between him and her? The daughter seemed to be able to read her mother's thoughts, and said, 'Mother, I can assure you with my telepathic machine that your intuition is completely wrong at the moment. But the grass roots will always be around, whether or not the stalk and the leaves wither and turn to wood. Battles in some Beirut or other will flare up when we least expect it, especially in the most peaceful of places.'

In the evening the daughter put on her anorak, even though it was warm and autumn had not yet started, and she walked out into the night with her Walkman, sat down in the shelter of the bank in front of the farm, and watched the sunset for a long time. She was probably listening to music or tunes which were well suited to the ruddy, awesome beauty of the evening. But she never sang along. She listened endlessly, but never sang along. The tunes did not lure song on to her tongue. Once her mother had said to the girl, out of the blue, 'She's not listening to pop music.'

The girl looked at her in surprise.

'She's not even listening to music,' the farmer's wife went on. 'She's listening to a tape and learning the third most widely spoken language in the world.'

'Really,' the girl blurted out. 'Why?'

'Because you've heard it said before, as she says herself, that the future lies in South America,' the woman said. 'For Iceland's sake I don't believe it, but the latest ideals claim there's no question about it.'

12

All of a sudden the daughter was constantly waving a telescope around, scanning the countryside with it. Her mother had a habit of taking it furtively down from the hook and repeatedly taking it out on to the steps and pointing it in all directions while twisting her body around, without leaving the spot where she was standing. The farmer, on the other hand, was in sole command of it in the evenings and looked through it discreetly out of the kitchen window by gently raising the pin at the bottom.

Once when the girl was sitting in the hallway, for some reason at home by herself with no one in the farmhouse but the silence, she took the telescope without permission and pointed it in all directions the way she had seen the others do. She had never looked through a telescope before and was startled when the farms that were near by but far away shot up into her eyes and slammed into her vision in a grey haze. At once she was filled with a sense of shame, because she could see someone standing outside on the steps at most of the farms, pointing a telescope at the others or in all directions.

What is everyone looking for; can they be spying on each other? she asked herself, and her heart began racing.

By sneaking a look through the telescope, the invisible had become visible, forced its way like a humiliating slap right into her chest and shoved her heart uncomfortably along with a rapid beat. No explanation had ever occurred to her mind of what it was the people on the farm were always looking for. Now she thought she realized that they were only checking on whether the others were looking at it, and the ones who were taking a peek were checking whether anyone was looking at them. She felt that she was under constant surveillance, that all the telescopes in the countryside were pointed at her and could even see into her and through her soul. This tranquil rural district on the edge of the drainage system on the plain was squirming with watchful eyes. After this, she was never alone. Someone was secretly monitoring her every movement from the distance, and she therefore preferred to be indoors, because something not unrelated to an evil god was constantly watching her.

With this discovery she became a telescope herself and began to keep a secret eye on the daughter, but the daughter was very wary and noticed this behaviour immediately, undoubtedly on her guard against other people in the local manner anyway.

'Why are you staring at me with those calf's eyes of yours?' she asked aggressively.

The girl became evasive, shy but pleased at her eyes being calf's eyes. It had no particular significance, apart perhaps from the fact that she would meet the same death as the calf then; that the daughter would cut her throat. Several times she imagined, in raptures just before she fell asleep, how her throat was cut and the blood spat out in all directions, filling the cups of the buttercups in the meadow, while the sun shone and made its beams stretch the blood out of her and turned a sunset red and threatening in the sky in the middle of the day until it rained it back in beams of light across the countryside and regained its normal colour. At this the girl grew wonderfully ecstatic before falling asleep, like the evening at the end of a sunny day.

If she played the same game somewhere during the day, the dusk repeatedly clouded her mind and turned ordinary objects strange, ignited a spirit within them or made them poisonous while the blood spurted out from her neck. One red drop fell into the open crown of each buttercup in the meadow, the bloody knife dropped to the ground from an invisible hand, her head dropped against a newspaper, sweeping her smooth hair out of her face and forming a blond circle around it. Everything grew tired and cocooned in a calm that yearned for sleep and night. She decided to say something at the very moment that she died, make a wish, perhaps not eternal life, but rather that she would enter an unbreakable scallop shell. The day seemed to make a similar wish the moment that the light waned, that in the evening it would acquire a shell that was continually darkening. She made a wish that from the shell of night a new, unfamiliar day would flow, and its soul would vanish from its closed eyes into the eye of another day inside a blue shell. Then she visualized the red snail of night. And on thinking such a thing, she decided to let her soul out through the wide-open eyes at the very moment she gave up the ghost, convinced that if her soul sneaked out of her backside she would have to hang around in hell ever after for her pains.

'My soul must not forsake me and leave my body through my arse to God,' she thought. Then he won't accept it. It will smell horrible, because of the naughty things I did, and he'll throw it away angrily and say, 'Why cometh this shitty soul unto me?' He never does anything dirty, he never does anything naughty. Then God says, curtly, 'Hey, bad woman, you've lived in perpetual filth, your soul stinks, even if you did wipe it with life on the farm.'

Never before had the girl contemplated anything about the nature of the soul until the farmhand began to tell her about its wonders, and now she felt convinced that at the moment of death it must sneak as a vapour through some bodily orifice. 'But what if it wants to leave through my slit?' she thought in terror and began to cry; then she had an idea and went around for several days plugged up with the cork from an empty cough mixture bottle she had stolen. In this way she went around under the influence of the slumber of death, until she thought it likely that the eyes were not only the mirror of the soul but also one of the cavities that the soul could easily leave by, no less than vision. 'And we travel to other planets at the speed of light and are born again in the form of a new baby. That's why women take such a long time to have babies and give birth, because the secret of life makes them wait for a human being to die on a distant planet so that its soul can enter at last the new one which is being born, because the baby is a light that grows within the woman; and the moment that the light of life goes out in one body out in the galaxy, it kindles just as quickly in another that might be countless light years away.' This is what she had heard the farmhand telling his diary, and that for this reason woman was the bearer of light.

The farmhand sometimes helped her to acquire some kind of faith. He told her that the devil took the soul if it accidentally left through the genitals or backside.

'Some people's souls are all over the place in their bodies while they live,' he said.

'How?'

'And when they die, they try to find their way out through these unclean places that we despise so much,' he answered. 'That's why hell is a sump of piss. Anyone who falls down through the hole to it in the middle of the night never gets back out, and will drown, no matter how furiously he calls out for help and tries to swim in the mire. Anyone who ends up in hell drowns in the pool of piss that has oozed from the souls of corrupted men.'

'It'd be repulsive too if your soul left through your nose or ears,' she said.

The farmhand agreed with her wholeheartedly. But he did not know where it would end up if it chose such an exit at the moment of death.

'Souls that fly out of people's noses when they sneeze probably end up on endless soul voyages, I suppose,' he said.

'What about your ears then?'

'They go to the dogs.'

The girl often racked her brains over such riddles, together with the farmhand who said, 'If we rack our brains so completely about eternity, we'll end up as missionaries in Africa.'

He asked her whether they shouldn't start practising preaching and begin by him revealing a new faith to the daughter. 'Yes, let's give it a try,' he said, and asked her once out of the blue, 'Listen, my girl, as an educated and worldly wise woman, do you know where the soul goes if it's sneezed out through the nose at the moment of death?'

'Into a handkerchief, the air, on to the back of your hand,' the daughter answered at once.

'I mean, if you give up the ghost by sneezing,' the farmhand said. 'Dying men don't usually wave handkerchiefs around.'

'Hey,' she said. 'The soul doesn't abandon the body all at once or in one piece, it fiddles around trying to beat a retreat out of the body from the moment we're born. You're dying the whole time you live. Death isn't the worst thing about death, but rather that your consciousness disappears at the same time, awareness of ourselves and others too. That's what we find most difficult to put up with. We don't want to stop knowing.'

She was sitting on the tractor, very scruffy as usual, as she gave this short speech. When she finished it she shrugged her shoulders with her body full of sun, but was upset at having unexpectedly said something she had never pondered before and undoubtedly originated from someone else. She took hold of her stomach, her belly was flat, and her eyes saddened slightly. Recently she had been looking at people in a different way from before; she had grown more distant from them and only went around in scruffy old clothes.

'Poor thing, the young maiden's become the foetus she had aborted, and that makes her body more beautiful and inaccessible than before; she's all the more desirable for it,' the farmhand had told the girl before he spoke to the daughter. 'It's because she's turned into the morning sun and evening sun at the same time.'

Now he walked away pensively from the daughter, who continued to drive around on the tractor, to no apparent purpose. Generally she was busily backing towards something, jerking the tractor back and forth or moving objects endlessly from place to place, carts and harvesters alike.

'I listened to her day and night and now I know that every day a part of another man dies within me, although I hardly feel it; I hereby quote almost verbatim the young lady who recently aborted her foetus,' the girl saw that the farmhand had written in his diary when she sneaked a look at it the following morning. 'Yet there is more besides which I have no idea is dying there. Some time I shall doubtless wake up to the fact that most aspects of me have died.'

He lay stretched out in the meadow with his arms stretched out and his legs spread when she read that in secret, and when she put the diary back down, went out and walked over to him, he raised

70

himself up merrily, held out his hand and led her around the meadow.

It was a Sunday, the farmer and his wife had driven off on some errand and the farmhand and the girl thought the daughter had gone with them, but then she darted round the corner of the house, dashed inside, came straight back with the telescope and stood on the steps for a long time. The girl saw that she pointed it at the mountain and the farm at its foot, although she swung it around in various directions for appearance's sake, wanting to conceal the fact by doing so when she noticed it. Then she sat down on one step and started patting the dog, raising the telescope occasionally and pointing it firmly at the mountain or swinging it in all directions.

The farmhand and the girl had lain down at the bottom of the bank. They were watching her and he said, 'A German girl who tames horses has turned up in the district. She works for a company that exports Icelandic horses. Now it turns out that no one in Iceland has ever sat a horse properly until now, so she's teaching young men and women the art of riding in that stables over there.'

He pointed down to the lowlands, far away where the mountain was close to the river. A newly built stables stood there, unpainted, and the sun glittered on the grey corrugated-iron roof.

'Now the farmer and his wife go there every Sunday to learn the right way to ride a horse from the German girl,' he added. 'A certain someone is learning how to ride with her too, that's why the wretch here has her telescope in the air all the time. Even educated people think there must be something mysterious and ticklish about the art of riding.'

'Why doesn't she learn too, then?' asked the girl.

'Some women think they don't need to learn that art, just men. They think it's in their blood how to sit properly on a tame horse!'

He broke off a piece of straw and tickled the girl behind her ear.

'Now thirty telescopes on the farms around here can see me "touching up a prepubescent child at the foot of a green hill in the sunshine" and soon the phones will start ringing and maybe tomorrow morning I'll be issued with a summons for attempted rape after sexual harassment of a girl on Sunday.'

He rolled over on to his back and snapped his teeth eagerly a couple of times at the sunshine and wind.

'Are you going to let yourself be raped when you're big?' he asked.

'Yes, if anyone can manage it,' she replied.

'Then you'd be doing other people's imaginations a great favour,' the farmhand said.

'How?' she asked.

He put on a mysterious expression and started tickling her ear and nose in turn.

'Then other people could have, for a while, a fraction of the relief with themselves that they yearn to have from others for the whole of their lives,' he said. 'It's the need for strength that does that.'

'Are you strong?'

'No, not enough. No one's strong enough.'

13

It was night and the girl woke up at someone entering the room, walking over to her bed and evaporating or vanishing. Extremely slowly and carefully she put her feet on the floor, so as not to frighten off the dream or drive it out of her mind, and she crept in this half-sleeping state after the invisible visitor out into the night, and chased him down to the river. Reaching there, she was startled awake by seeing the daughter sitting motionless on the riverbank.

The girl thought that the daughter had really come into her room and woken her up into a new dream and led her through it for some specific purpose down to the place by the river where the water was relatively calm and resembled a wide, slow current.

The white, cold water passed by in the grey night. The girl was going to lie down and hide before she came right up to the daughter, but she seemed to have an intuition about her presence, looked over her shoulder and saw her immediately. She said nothing, but gestured to the girl to come over, but instead of obeying she turned back to the farmhouse as if disappearing from an incomprehensible or bad dream.

After this she often crept out at night, drawn by a mysterious and sad yearning to find out whether the daughter was always sitting by the river, and she always saw her sitting there. Then she would sit down on the ground in her underwear too, far behind her, so that she could watch her profile. She waited, but it was not a wait for anything special. She just waited with her soul neutral, without waiting. They were aware of each other but did not exchange words, and always at the end when the daughter raised her arm and gestured silently to her to come, instead of obeying she would return to the farmhouse as if from a bad dream.

On the way over the meadow she was on the verge of tears, without any sorrow but rather because she felt she was sitting there herself, invisible, in the same place by the same river that women have sat beside in the vague tragedy of their nature for all time, and would sit there in the night of the sex that gives birth and kills for as long as the world lasts, without knowing why, and without it being their will or them being sad; instead, they were just sitting there alone by the river in the chill of night.

In the night, while she was waiting behind the daughter, she mentally moved the mountain, as she sometimes did in the day, so that she could see the route home, even though she could not see all the way there.

The daughter stared interminably out at the river and paid no attention to the girl, even though she had gestured to her to come over. Probably she wanted the river suddenly to flood its banks, snatch her up and take her away, because the girl had once felt a not dissimilar sensation, but relating to the earth: that arms suddenly came up out of a ditch, grabbed her by the shoulders and dashed her down forcefully on to the compact soil on its banks. This greedy yearning drove her upriver one night, and when she was out of sight she fetched a polished pebble from the shallow water at its bank and placed it, wet, soft and cold, first between her legs and then on her navel. After that she slept with it on her, although she was frightened that someone would come up to her in her sleep, dash off her quilt, see the pebble and start laughing and shout loud enough for everyone to hear, 'She sleeps with a pebble on her stomach!'

For several nights her dreams turned menacing and good. The relief at waking from sleep and being alive was all the more pleasant, the more that the torture of the dreams increased. Beautiful dreams were different, disappointments awoke if she woke up from them in the middle of the night, because life was much worse than they were, but better than the bad ones. She started to wonder whether the daughter slept in her room with a stone on her stomach too, cool and soft from the river, a flat, grey pebble that water had flowed over and stroked endlessly until she had taken it away.

She did not know. By day neither of them mentioned their nocturnal travels, but the girl racked her brains about what it could be that drove them out to look either at the river or over towards the mountain.

On a sandspit by the bank was a little boat that could be rowed across the river. The farmhand did so sometimes at weekends. He went alone on his trips across the river and the girl watched him going, the way he rowed in the still and calm water along the side of the bank, then thrust himself out into the current and let the boat be swept downriver in the middle of the stream and disappeared around a meander, until he returned much later and rowed upriver in the calm water on the other bank.

'Why did you do that?' she asked.

'Just to get carried along with the current,' he answered. 'It does me good to sit in a little boat in a strong current, pull in the oars and let myself float away, preferably to sea. But that's too far away, the boat would have broken apart and sunk before it could make it there.'

The boat seemed to serve no other purpose, but it was used to fetch the blue dun mare, which had a tendency to bolt. It had been bought from a farm some way off on the other side of the river, and even though the farm stood out of sight behind some foothills, the horses came down from there occasionally to the riverbank and neighed. If the mare saw them it would whimper back as if unable to forget its native haunts. And one day that otherwise calm and stubborn animal had disappeared. Usually the farmer rowed with his daughter to fetch it, when he had the time.

'It's just good sport, rowing,' he said when they returned.

He seemed pleased at having come back into contact with the old days, when everything had to be fetched from across the river. The daughter was contented too, and not at all dazed by the exposure but bright-voiced instead, and she said she could never remember ever having left home except when she met people of her own age, the daughters of the farmer who had owned the mare. They had always stayed put with their parents and were cheerful like all people who have come to accept the fact that the path of life extends only as far as a certain place, a destination which their voyage here on earth had reached long ago. At the end of it, the greatest fool's errand of life would disappear into the grave one day, but they did not care even if they found nothing.

'The sisters remember various things, yes, so many things that I've forgotten,' she said. 'I'm starting to think that going to college and studying is an easy way to forget, at least certain things, like your origins. Their minds hardly go beyond the range of their horse and cows. Their occasional trips out at weekends in the car are merely to celebrate for a while, maybe spend a night with a man when they get the itch. Then that's over and it's back home as if nothing had ever happened. I wish I were made that way. I've much too good a memory in all respects to be able to shake off the dust without feeling pain for months or even years afterwards.'

She told her mother this while she was stroking the mare. It was a well-built horse, stubborn and sluggish. Really it served no useful purpose, apart from being ridden where you couldn't go in the car because of marshes and wetlands. If they went for a ride on Sundays, the girl was put on the mare.

'She's stubborn,' said the farmer, 'but so loyal that she wouldn't shy, throw you off her back and gallop off, even if the end of the world were nigh and she could avoid it by running away.'

Usually the girl was sent on its back with coffee, too, if they were making hay in the part of the field that the car could not negotiate properly. Then she rolled back and forth on its back until she got a stitch. The cups in the basket would rattle uncomfortably to the rhythm of the stitch. The mare's back was so broad that it was almost impossible to fall off. In the farmhouse there were many photographs of children on her back. Five children were sitting there in one. In the photo album there were more photographs of the mare than of any other horse. Sometimes it would stop unexpectedly and there would be no way to make it budge from the spot. The girl dangled her legs but the mare would not move. It hung around there so long that the girl thought she had fallen asleep. Then she would be on the verge of tears, in desperation at the animal's incomprehensible behaviour, but just as the tears were about to break forth the mare would lumber away. The girl tried to resort to pretending to cry, just to trick the mare, but the mare could feel that this was just pretending; a ruse directed at it, and then it stood even longer than usual by way of punishment.

'That fine horse enters a charmed state without the slightest warning, to contemplate life and human existence,' the farmhand said. 'Be on your guard. One day it could turn to stone. If you feel something like it congealing, be quick to leap off its back, otherwise the substance that is turning it to stone will seep through you from behind and change you into a stone troll. And those are awful women.'

In her mind's eye she saw the mare hardening and her own marrow congealing, so that they turned into a statue by the roadside, and tourists came to look at them, and the farmhand said, 'Once upon a time that was a real mare with a real girl on her back.'

It did not make her happy to hear the farmhand's endless stupid stories which she never completely understood, they were so peculiar; sometimes his eyes filled with tears of joy, when he forgot himself for love of their content and seemed as if he would never stop. That struck her as the strangest thing of all.

'Why are you telling that nonsense?' she asked.

'I have to spin some yarn and confide it to my diary: that I've met a stranger who told me this in this ignorant place,' he answered. 'My diary's the only sweetheart I have.'

On saying this his expression turned so solemn that the girl patted him. Then he became silly and after that very glassy-eyed, stared out at nothing and asked her to pat him again and tell him if she thought of any nonsense to tell.

'I also collect funny stories so that I can tell them to a sweetheart and charm her when I go off courting to find myself a prospective wife,' he said with a childish laugh.

The cows would sometimes forget themselves in the evenings. Then the girl rode the mare to look for them and fetch them. The daughter took a colour photograph of her on the mare's back, with the sunset in the background above the mountain. The girl was impatient and wanted to see the photo straight away, and often asked whether it had been sent off to be developed.

'No,' answered the daughter. 'Don't worry, you won't leave the film. All the children who come here in the summer are supposed to have a photo of themselves for as long as it lasts.'

Then she said that the photo would be stuck into the album and new children would come and browse through it and want to know who the others had been.

'The years go by like that and in the end such a long time will go by that no one will remember any more what children they were,' said the daughter. 'Then someone will say, "Oh, she was just an ordinary girl, then." You who are a definite girl now, such a size, maybe you'll be some dead and long-forgotten old woman then, and everyone will ask, "Do you reckon she's still alive?" No one will know. You'll just be forgotten.'

At these words the girl grew thoughtful, although she did not think about anything in particular except that there was something pressing on her eyes and she didn't understand time and how could she turn into nothing in particular over the years. She tried to contemplate this and find an answer to fix herself upon, but within a short while she had started thinking about something else. In the end she didn't even know what she had been thinking about in the first place. Even the day before yesterday was largely forgotten and it didn't matter, the day today was just as good or equally bad all the same, and what did it matter anyway if everything turned into the past in the end and everyone had forgotten the names of what had been necessary to remember at a specific time?

Whenever she was disconsolate and the farmhand saw it, he placed his hand warmly on her back, between her shoulderblades, and she tried to tell him what he knew much better than she did anyway, and he always said it before she had found the words to do so. In the evening he sat at the desk writing his diary and said, when she was watching him, 'By far the best thing is to forget the past. All the same I advise you to start keeping a diary.'

'What for?'

'To show your boyfriend when you get one. Then he can get to know you. I'm always entering my biography, my life and me into my diary for a prospective wife to browse through. "Now I'll surely get a sweetheart before I finish this volume," I say to myself when there are only a few pages left. I do that to magic sweethearts to me. They won't be able to bear watching the pages getting filled but my wishes going unfulfilled! No. The volumes fill up and no sweetheart enters my life. I pile up in writing, my biography grows but the possibilities diminish. All I fill up is pages. I gain countless diaries but no sweetheart. Then I say to myself, "Well, if you can't give your sweetheart your diaries, then eternity can just have them as a present. It's no worse."'

Having said this the farmhand moved his head, smiling. It was as if he did not really believe a single word of what he had been saying. That is why he smiled at the end.

'All the same, it's better to confide in letters rather than other people,' he said. 'I'm most afraid that when I finally do get a sweetheart I'll have written so much about myself that when I hand her the stack and say, "Well, dear, if you really want to get to know your prospective husband, then have a careful read of these private papers, word by word," and then she'll say, "Oh, God Almighty, I can't be bothered to read that load of stuff, it won't be worth it. I'm breaking off our engagement and I'd prefer to marry a dishonourable liar who doesn't need to produce testimonies or written evidence for God knows what."'

The girl asked why he didn't make the daughter his sweetheart.

'Because I could do it so easily, now that the cygnet is licking her wounds after the last one,' answered the farmhand. 'The moment she'd got me for a sweetheart she'd have wanted a different one, and I'd have wanted a different one from her, having really got the taste for sweethearts and because in our own respective ways we'd have acted too fast about an emotional situation that wouldn't work out in the end because it would have been too easy to get out of.'

'I don't understand,' said the girl.

'I bet you don't,' he said. 'But don't you always want another sweet when you've just had a nice tasty one?'

'Yes,' she answered.

'It's the same with sweethearts. And that's why it's by far the best thing not to have any at all. Then you won't get mouth rot.'

14

Although the local weather made the summer sunny, it sometimes swept clouds into the sky, probably to prevent the days becoming empty in too much uniformity of brightness and dryness. The clouds broke up the monochrome blue at appropriate intervals, so that showers could always be expected after a suitably long dry spell, and the earth rose up to life anew in warm damp.

When it rained or showered everyone popped inside the farmhouse, leaving nothing outside in the realm of nature apart from the rain. Nature was outside in the realm of nature. And because of the long dry spells nature turned raw blue and the rain wetter than usual rain. It was only the chickens that roamed around in the rain, shaking the clear raindrops from their red combs. The girl watched this out of the window or in the farmhouse doorway, if she wanted to feel the moist chill on her legs from the rain as it beat on the earth outside, to smell the scent of the once brittle grass and earth when they awoke, but at the same time the warmth that emanated from inside the house and played across her back.

The most fun of all was during downpours, when the rumbling filled the air and the drops pounded on the cabbage, beating it like little soft, green drums.

But the greatest noise was from the corrugated iron on the roof of the barn. She went in there to listen when it was raining hardest, lay down in the hay and disappeared into the ponderous din which was like endless sleep and calm plummeting down from the heavens. The rumbling made the hay strange and drier than it actually was, and the scent of it grew heavier, pungent, sour and mixed with the wet smell of the soil outside and merged with the aromatic sense of well-being within her. But nothing else descended from the heavens to lie down softly on top of her and press her firmly into the hay, nothing, only the first isolated beating of raindrops and then afterwards a growing murmur which in the end became a downpour with countless variations.

The rain generated tranquillity everywhere. There was drowsiness inside the house. The food became heavy in the stomach. And the people slept and slept. The house gave off a scent of drenched dreams, when the people there gave each other cryptic glances which swam in a longing slumber under heavy eyelids. The farmhand groped into the air for the daughter when he went into his room to sleep. He was so tired after his labours that when he woke up after his afternoon nap he was still asleep even when he loped around or sat at the table rubbing his face. He talked intoxicated nonsense with peculiar giggles over the lunchtime coffee. The daughter watched him, rigid, and smoked. The farmer nipped in to drink his coffee but said nothing, popped out to the door with his telescope, looked around and saw only the fuzzy land beneath the pouring rain.

Then the farmhand slipped out into the barn and fell asleep with all his limbs stretched out. He lay like a gigantic X in the hay. When the girl was sent out with a bowl of leftovers for the chickens she went into the barn to see the way he was sleeping. She was holding the empty bowl in her hands and began to tap with her fingers, then drum lightly with her nails on the bottom, while the farmhand slept like a gigantic X in the hay. For her, all the days were alike. She was continually made to do little chores. Now she no longer put on her black raincoat, but draped it loosely over her head, paralysed by sleepiness at hearing the sound of the rain on the waterproof material. At this moment she was not under the raincoat, nor in the barn, but rather a dry package inside a black membrane which concealed her and the world. She was a chick in a black egg with a black shell and she waited for someone to break the shell so that she could crawl out to life and other people, while the farmhand lay like a gigantic X and slept a gentle sleep, and she watched him and tapped lightly with her nails on the bottom of the bowl.

Then the rain cleared up, the barn roof fell silent and sounds awoke outside in the realm of nature. The birds began chirping anew. Cars could be seen driving along the road through the countryside. The farmer came out to the doorway, wide awake, with his telescope. The phone started ringing. The farmhand pulled the arms of his X up to his sides, got to his feet, shuffled out of the barn and said while stretching comfortably, 'I wonder how many farmers' daughters have got pregnant while that long shower was making the grass grow?'

The girl did not listen to him, she was watching the birds out in the meadow. Now she had stopped feeling they were like brown rocks that some angry spirit had tossed up from the earth. Earlier that summer she had seen them running along either in front of or behind her. They stopped, took a look, darted off, were always waiting, seeing her coming and playing a trick on her, sometimes with a low whine, sometimes spreading out their wings and beating the earth with them furiously. That was the way birds complained.

She knew that these rituals meant that they probably had nests somewhere, but she had never found them in the marshland, no matter how much she looked. There was so much vegetation, the chicks small and doubtless the same colour as the earth. But even though it was past hatching time and the chicks were probably just becoming fledglings by now, she still had a feeling that she had accidentally trodden on one and squashed it, sending the bloody pulp spurting out beneath her feet, mixed with the russet mud of the marsh. A shudder ran through her every time she had the notion that she was walking on a murderer's feet.

The clouds rolled on along the days and weeks, in varying hues of greyish white out on the horizon, but sometimes they crept slowly up along the firmament and filled it up to the zenith when the brightness was starting to irritate the eyes. The river, too, seemed to have flowed up into the arc of the skies, and at that moment it wrapped itself in the guise of fog around the brow of the mountain. There it swept onwards in slender, pointed streaks, its current strong in the wind, until the southwesterly wind ripped it to shreds and swung it down to its course once more. At the same time, the mountain lit up. The river disappeared back into the river, the sun drove away the rain and changed to shine, the earth dried, the breeze shook drops from the leaves and the dogs barked. The girl stretched out her palm to feel the cold kiss of the last raindrop. The daughter came out to hurry on to the machines, but the farmhand became worked up and acted idiotically when he noticed her from the barn doorway and called after her in a booming voice, 'The summer in your eyes is like a dream and the wind grows lecherous in your dress, though your thighs can handle it and you drive it away with . . . God knows what.'

The daughter roared with laughter at him and pulled a face.

'You're always a bit perky after your afternoon nap,' she said mockingly.

In a short while she had disappeared on the tractor, only her unmelodic singing could be heard like shouts through the whirring of the engine, out of sight of the farm.

The farmhand looked at the girl with a grin and whispered insinuatingly, 'My dear, do you know about the rain that rains on itself and . . . ?'

He looked away from her with a shameful face and fell silent.

The girl proceeded on her way indoors and sat down on her bed, wondering about something. It was then that she suddenly remembered going off some time with her parents to an unfamiliar place, down by the sea. Now she could clearly visualize the black sand on the shore, rock outcrops and puddles. The smell was like after a shower and she had lain down on a rock and drunk water from a puddle. There was a vague sandy taste to the water. Just as she had put her lips to it and found the vague taste she noticed a little flower growing in a crevasse in the rock. A rainbow rose over the black sand. There were no plants there, nothing but outcropping rocks and that flower, but she found a red shell as well.

'It's a scallop shell,' her mother said. 'Those shells are always pink.'

Then her father said, 'Listen,' and she could hear the sea, and the sound was joined to the reddish-pink shell. And now she could hear the same murmuring from the sea, as she knelt hunched up on the bed, in exactly the same way she had long ago in time immemorial, and had found the pink shell so far away from the sea. She closed her eyes and could hear the playing of what she thought was the pale blue harp of the ocean, whose resonance stretched in through the land and whose song meandered along the whole road she had taken that spring; it moved probingly up hills and down into gullies and jumped over bridges, all the way into her chest at an endless distance from its source, so she mentally stretched out in the darkness for the flower in the crevasse only to find that she had dozed off sitting down on her bed.

'Do you know about the rain that rains on itself and . . . ?' she repeated after the farmhand.

For a while she was close to tears at not having reached the flower with the hands that she was gradually losing that summer. Instinctively she put them to her chest because her heart was racing and then she was seized by fear: she was starting to grow breasts. She caught her breath in wonder and horror. It was just as if those breasts had grown on her with the shower of rain that had come that afternoon. She crept out to the toilet to examine this in the mirror and be able to scratch herself without anyone seeing. When she saw a tiny redness which contrasted with her white body she went weak at the knees and sat down on the chair beside the bath tub. Suddenly she was afraid that she might have become pregnant too, just from seeing the farmhand lying like a gigantic X in the hay. For that reason she carefully pulled down her knickers, on the verge of falling into a faint, took a shy peep between her legs and tried to have a shit, but could not. Her nipples sat still on her white breasts but may have been slightly red from struggling to sprout.

The sound of voices could be heard through the door and she stopped examining herself. The daughter had come back from the machines and she knocked a few times without the girl answering. Then she said to someone, 'The country show's being held this weekend, I've just heard. Open up, girl!' she called.

The girl took a swift look at herself and could not see anything abnormal about her body.

85

'It's sheer imagination,' she thought, quickly pulled her dress back down over herself and tried to put on a natural expression.

'Open up, girl!' the daughter called. 'I know what you're doing in there.'

15

For the rest of the week the girl kept a constant watch on the blue dun mare, afraid that it would suddenly get the idea of bolting just before the country show and the farmer wouldn't have time to row over the river to fetch it, so that she would either have to stay at home or go there by car, because she wouldn't be able to ride there with the others.

She knew it was the general custom for people to go to the show on horseback and leave their cars behind, unless old people were taken along to listen to the open-air church service.

When the weekend drew near everyone started checking the saddles, straps and bridles. Inside the house a comfortable smell of leather surged up and then the girl noticed, which she had never paid any attention to before, that most of the objects indoors were made of plastic, even the flowers. The daughter brushed the saddles and polished every strap in the hallway, but also did the same with the old whips in the sitting room and examined the silver ornament on them with great interest.

'At last I can get on the machines,' the farmhand said in a jolly mood. 'I'm not the young lady's pageboy any more. But what a beautiful silver whip she's got!'

The daughter spent the day busying herself with the horses. At mealtimes she recalled, in a lofty recitation, all the horses that had been on the farm since as far back as she could remember, naming them all and describing them in detail. She also took out the horse album and showed photographs of them and read from *The History of Horses* which had been written by two generations of her family. In the hallway she hung up the poster that she had bought with pictures of Icelandic horses on it and descriptions of their colours. When this was over the farmhand always said the same thing, 'Steeds are clearly healthy for certain souls.'

The farmer did not seem to know how to respond to this repetitive comment of his, but said, 'In general the countryside and everything in it has a healthy effect on people, men and women, young and old.'

'Not the women,' said the farmhand curtly.

'It depends on how you look at it,' said the farmer in an important tone of voice.

'You can only look at it in one way,' said the farmhand.

'It completely depends on who you're talking about,' said the farmer's wife, and the subject was dropped.

In the evenings the farmer went out riding with his daughter to put the steeds through their paces and break them in for the show. She had her Walkman with her and the headphones clasped over her ears, and the farmhand said he thought it was a shame that there were no miniature Japanese televisions yet to fix on the saddle stop for people on horseback. The daughter made no reply but said, to change the subject, 'That German girl's giving a display of the art of riding at the show. It's said she studied at the famous riding school in Vienna where steeds greet people with their front legs like well-trained dogs. But they can't make them fetch their master's slippers or riding boots in their mouths, when they see him enter the stables; they consider it below their equine dignity.'

Her parents pretended not to have heard what she said. Then she looked at the farmhand with her eyes boggling and exhaled with a heavy jet of air through her nose, implying that they had no sense of humour. He had gone off in the jeep one evening to watch the German girl taming horses in the paddock and said he was more surprised at how quick she had been to learn Icelandic from him in one evening than he to learn her equestrian skills.

'The only thing she does unquestionably well is to make the horses lift their feet quickly, like gigantic spiders with long, spindly legs that grope out into the air for purchase,' he said.

'Really?' said the daughter.

'They go half rampant with their front legs like certain types of spider that are straying away from their webs,' the farmhand said meaningfully.

'Is that supposed to be an art?' asked the daughter.

'It depends on the way you look at the art of riding,' the farmhand answered.

'Maybe in Vienna, but not here in Fludasel,' the farmer said curtly.

'In days of old the heroes' horses stampeded out of the clouds in peals of thunder, but nowadays they canter along on riding trips and at the most they foam at the mouth and champ at their bits, but the mares are easy to handle, they obey and know how to amble,' said the farmhand.

The farmer's wife was of the opinion that they ought to ban all export of Icelandic horses.

'Icelandic horses ought to be for the Icelanders alone,' she said. 'Maybe foreigners do sit their horses better than we do, artistically I mean, but they'll never be part of their souls. That German girl teaches a way of riding that's good for the spine and the small of the back, but foreigners don't exactly belong on the back of our dear horses.'

'Other farmers around here don't seem to agree with you,' said the farmhand. 'They're always selling their untamed horses to be exported and tamed and they get good money for it.'

'Making money has nothing to do with me and my opinions,' the farmer's wife said firmly.

There were five neighbouring farms in a cluster and they would have formed a kind of hamlet, had they not each been built on their respective hillocks, all of which resembled huge, domed, green, upturned buckets of varying sizes, with fairly smooth and flat bottoms. The houses were built on them, and the outhouses farther down on the slopes at a considerable distance, to help stop the flies that preyed on the animals from flying in and filling the rooms. It was not very far from one farm to the next, but there was virtually no contact; instead, everyone kept an eye on everyone else and all traffic through the family telescope. They deliberately avoided pointing it at the farmhouse door in full view of everyone else, but aimed it through the lower panel of the kitchen window instead. On the other hand, it was pointed unremittingly in full view of everyone from the steps towards distant farms. For some reason, people there were always celebrating their fiftieth birthdays that summer with big parties lasting into the night; and either they did not invite the right people or it was strange to see some of the people there.

The day they rode off to the country show, the neighbours' quarrels about fences disappeared and so did their resentment that the cows might have grazed on other grass and in other places than they were supposed to. People set off on horseback from all the farms at more or less the same time. Each party rode off from its respective home in a crocodile down the hill. Then they grouped up on the road which lay smooth and asphalted over the marshland right beside the river. The people exchanged merry greetings and went in almost a single group while making lively but disjointed conversation about nothing in particular, as if they had ridden away from everything: the past, daily drudgery, work, the animals and the earth, and into the promised land where endless merriment and prospective unbridledness reigned supreme. The farms were left behind on their own in the sunshine on their hillocks, resembling toy houses or children's drawings, except the black smoke from chimneys was missing. Only the girl felt left out and could not keep her mind on anything but the horse's rough back, and tried to avoid the worst jolts by standing firm in the stirrups to air her backside. Because of the sore pains in her body she never got into rhythm with the others and rode far behind them. The children from the other farms, who did not need to work because their parents paid for them to stay there for the summer, had been shuttled ahead of them in jeeps, together with frail old people.

The farther that the girl gradually fell behind the others and the pain in her body increased, the more she became like a knot on a hard plank in an unknown world full of sun, full of dust on the riding track along the side of the wet marshland with its grasses that peeped calmly up from the glittering tarns. She was so totally alone in the tranquillity, when she could no longer hear the others and a cloud of dust covered them on the riding track alongside the main road, that she could almost tangibly feel the presence of the unfamiliar, and she felt so good that she even feared having to join the company of other people at the end of her journey. She was almost lost in the fuzzy world of unfamiliarity when she saw the cloud of dust from the riding party thin out, fall down to the track and clear from the daughter who was waiting for her on the road. She was riding her trotting, uneasy horse round in circles on a little patch of the raised, asphalted road without looking over at the girl. But as soon as the girl saw the daughter, there was nothing else for her to do but head towards her and gratefully join her company. And when she rode up to her horse, she dissolved in rejoicing and submission. The daughter said only, 'Try to keep with the party and never get left behind, otherwise you'll just get lost. You won't find your way there by yourself.'

Having said this, she rode down from the road to the riding track and galloped away.

The earth jumped, the mountains tossed. Everything was unclear and moving before the girl's eyes: up and down, smeared and shredded. The mountains sploshed around like thick porridge as countless needles went through her from the rough horse. The sunshine shook about like yellow juice in a bottle. She gave a low whine with her mouth half open to ease the pain; and she thought they'd never reach the venue of the show. The daughter variously rode way ahead of her, got lost in the spray of dust by the mountainside, or stopped and waited for her, then rode on again and said impatiently, bored by her own helpfulness, 'Do try to keep your butt up with the others.'

They rode on endlessly like this, although the girl hoped that the daughter would eventually leave her alone and the horse would take her, no matter where. Nor did she care if they continued until kingdom come and never reached any destination. It was as if the daughter had heard her wish, for she stopped waiting for her and spurred her horse in the direction that the others had ridden. In a short while she had vanished into the dust on the riding track, and when it thinned out and fell to the ground again, she and the horse were nowhere to be seen; nor the other people.

The girl was alone on her horse.

16

The daughter suddenly cantered up on her horse. The girl had not noticed and thought she had been dozing or had fallen asleep against its neck with her face buried in its coarse mane. She gave a start when the horse broke into a gallop. She was thrown around, looked up, saw who had arrived and giggled, sore, her head bowed low, and tried for a while to ride alongside the daughter who drove her horse ahead, striking it occasionally with her whip.

'No,' she pleaded meekly, because she was so stiff and sore that she regretted having gone there.

They caught up with the others who had stopped for a short rest by the riverbank and were sitting in a group there, watching them and laughing at them with their mouths full of food.

When they all remounted the horses, light grey streaks of showers had appeared over the mountain where the show was to be held in a green cirque which sloped towards the south. The bare and barren mountaintop stooped towards the flatlands as if the scalp had been cut from its head and stretched down towards the south. There it formed a horseshoe-shaped cirque which ended on a strip of flat ground that stretched to the bank of one of the two rivers. At the edge of the plain the flat ground undulated, with low dunes at first, followed by fairly high hills, then mountains and the highlands and interior pastures farthest inland.

People could be seen flocking to the venue on horseback, from all the neighbouring districts. Cars left the main road in clouds of dust and along a track which led to the flat ground. The people farthest off disappeared occasionally into dark, bluish showers of rain. Then the sun peeped back out and swept them westwards with its beams of light.

'You should make an effort never to let others leave you behind,' the daughter said to the girl as she struck her horse mightily with her whip and broke into a canter.

She rode away from her and disappeared with the rest of the group into the streaks of showers not far ahead.

The girl was by herself on the road again. The horse gradually slowed down once more and began to trot. It was not in a hurry, it clearly knew the way and knew where it was heading, there was no rush, the show would last until the evening.

The panorama spread out all the more as she rode on at her leisure on the sunny side of the showery patch, and she heard the peals of thunder from inside the black. Everything was silvery, the earth and the sky were entwined with lakes and clouds. In the distance the lakes seemed to rise in a shimmering upwelling towards the clouds and the sun cast a clear yellow hue on their edges.

The horse had stopped. It stood completely still in the silence of the sky and the earth which light clouds of steam were rising from in the sunshine. Occasionally the silence was broken and the earth by the roadside made a peculiar gurgle when bubbles of air rose up in various places through the marshland.

The girl leaned forward on her horse and half dozed as it slowly set off, and she felt as though she were travelling on a brown, warm ship which was comfortably sailing a choppy sea on its way out to something of whose end she had no idea. The smell of the horse played around her nostrils and the occasional fly buzzed. Now she was indifferent to everything, when she stretched forward on the horse, buried her face deep into its mane and grasped with both hands around its ears, feeling how they moved stiff, wriggling and gentle in her palms, like those of a mysterious creature.

When they finally reached the venue, everyone had unsaddled the horses and let them loose into the paddock. At that very moment, a girl rode up along with a swarm of young men who were accompanying her or following her.

'Oh, there's the German girl,' someone said with reverence.

The girl rode in front, serious, as if concerned with nothing but herself, her riding style and the horse, which lifted its front legs unusually high, moving them rapidly as if limbering itself up with great dignity but at the same time gliding onwards at a quick gallop. Its legs were curved forwards in arcs as it touched its hoofs gently on the earth for an instant, like a nimble spider running over a hot clump of moss. It was somehow vainglorious, this horse which rolled its eyes and curled its mane, with its head tucked down and its mouth foaming with white froth against its chest. It gave the impression of wanting to butt something or bite through its own throat from inner frenzy but was unable to because of the girl controlling it. That was why it was foaming at the mouth.

'Well, the art of riding seems to involve teaching an ordinary horse an abnormal or idiotic gait,' said the farmer's wife.

'No, that's genuinely beautiful,' the daughter said drily. 'You can see how something ordinary has been stylized and made exceptional through good grooming. That's the trick.'

'Really,' said her mother. 'So don't we know anything about horses any more?'

'You don't think about anything except what the horse is useful for, old peasant sentimentality and being able to go where you want on it.'

'Maybe you notice a horse better if it's like that, with a curly mane or all shifty, galloping along bent double,' said her mother. 'It looks like a horse that wishes it could turn into a galloping seashell.'

'That's just the point,' said the farmer. 'The animal's kept under tension, it feels compulsion, it's made nervous and that produces what's called beautiful movements.'

They watched the girl's riding for a while.

One of her male entourage greeted them when he rode past. Instead of returning his greeting directly, the farmer and his wife gave a sideways glance at the daughter. She responded to the greeting by waving merrily and clicking her fingers, and he swung out his hand, caught the click in his open palm, closed his fingers around it and kept it in his clenched fist.

'Bravo!' the daughter called out with a sarcastic laugh, low and purring.

'It's like performing dogs,' said a woman from the next farm.

The German girl had started making her horse walk backwards, snort and squat with irregular jerks, as if it were about to take a shit doggy-fashion or sit down on an invisible chair or throne. Instantly it stretched out again and started to rear, waving its front legs in the air, either in turn or almost in synchronization. When it did so she leaned forward on its neck and gave it free rein, so that it gaped into the air for a moment then darted forward, heading for a liberty that she promptly dispelled by making it canter prettily. She was wearing white jodhpurs, a tapered black jacket, polished riding boots and a black peaked cap.

'Anyone would think she'd come here to show off her own tricks,' someone said.

The men watched her suspiciously, attentively, their smiles concealing a hint of inferiority but at the same time a certain eagerness. When they set their horses at a gallop it was to make them speed lightly low over the ground, almost touching it. They pinned the horses beneath them with their legs, rode leaning forward over their necks, while the German girl sat her horse differently; she made it stylized and other-worldly, transformed it into a substance that was flesh and blood but racked with yearning for immateriality and flight.

'Yes, that might be a fine riding style for German industrialists or theatrical people from Reykjavík who are building the horse stock up again, but not for us farmers. It'll be a long time before we turn our horses into arty-farty playthings,' people said sarcastically, yet in such a way that they could feel how farmers had surely lost their grasp on the horse for ever and been given jeeps instead, because when all was said and done they had never had the faintest idea about riding-horses, only about pack-horses, and had never understood the horse's yearning for its substance to fly out into fiction and myth. They had merely made it their most needed servant, but not a companion in any other form than with the earthy inspiration of traditional verse, not the abstract yearning of the spirit for beauty and stylized dignity.

For this reason they turned away, rather grumpy, and did not want to watch the performance. Instead they stomped over the hummocky grass towards the tournament area.

A few poorly dressed kids stayed huddled there, blue with the cold, staring at the German girl. They had started gulping down fizzy drinks and were amusing themselves by belching. Sometimes they would leap into the air from sheer boredom and land in a patch of dirt, kicking with their feet or splashing each other with mud. They seemed to be holding a separate children's sports day before the real one began with the big heroes who kept themselves to one side and were furiously warming up or limbering their knees up on the field below, while a young lad strewed something resembling white flour in alternate straight and circular stripes on to the sports pitch. Between the straight and long stripes were the running tracks, while the circular ones were for the throwing events.

On seeing the athletes, many of the people unconsciously tried to assume a nimble and athletic air. But the old women said one after another, with a snort, 'Well, you couldn't get my body to do that, there'd be no point in trying at all.'

All the same, they looked on in enchantment at the exercises of the well-trained, supple-limbed athletes, perhaps thinking in the silence that this would give their bodies vigour anew to spend the afternoon hidden away in the hollows.

17

While she was waiting for the show to be declared open, the girl did not know what to do. People were strolling restlessly around the showground, exchanging short greetings or calling out hello to each other. Everyone knew everyone else here, for sure, but she knew no one apart from the people she had come with from the farm. They left her to herself and immediately joined the others, so that she was left out, was forgotten and had somehow lost her purpose because the other people were celebrating.

Then the show was declared open and the fact that speeches were made helped improve the situation slightly, because they packed the people together in silence and in a specific place. She stood pinned inside the crowd, saw nothing, heard little, but because of the warmth from their bodies she did not feel quite so much left out. The movement, the futile roaming around slopes and fields, was by far the worst part, and so was meeting other people, not knowing whether she ought to greet them or try to join a group of people she was not acquainted with.

She wandered hesitantly into the marquee where coffee was being sold. At the entrance a woman was standing over a shoebox full of money and notes which were so crumpled that they seemed to be wriggling and trying to make their way out of it. The woman asked, 'Who do you belong to?'

Just as quickly she seemed to have forgotten the question and had no interest in the answer, because she rushed away from the box to fiddle with something behind a sheet which was pulled over one of the corners of the marquee, where coffee was being made and cakes were being arranged on plates. A considerable noise was coming from there.

The girl ran her eyes over the countryside beyond the edge of the marquee: the rivers, the mountains; and the yellowish light from the tightly woven canvas of the tent made the sun, which was shining through it at that moment, stand out illuminated or in a kind of artificial corona, while the landscape outside was green in normal sunlight. In the state of mind that was kindled within her then she sensed that her parents were a vast distance away and doubtless either dead or non-existent, leaving her as a yellowish unreal girl in a coffee marquee in strange surroundings, so she replied, 'No one.'

Then she saw that the woman was no longer sitting at the shoebox, so she waited absolutely still in the light until the woman returned, pressed the notes firmly down into the box with the palm of her hand and asked, 'What do you want?'

'I don't belong to anyone,' the girl said.

The woman gave her a quick look, before she started calling out to the women behind the sheet at the far end of the marquee, and said absent-mindedly, 'Well, stay outside then.'

The girl obeyed at once and went out. There was no one she knew outside and she went on roaming from one group to the next. 'If I owned a horse I could go and show it to other people,' she thought and stomped over the rough ground towards the paddock. Several old men were standing there, sizing up the horses and telling tales of the exploits of living or long-dead horses. And outside the paddock a few young lads were hanging around, clearly drunk, on horseback. They planned to sit like that without dismounting for the duration of the show but drinking there at their leisure instead.

'The best place to get boozed up is on horseback,' one of them said and they all started laughing.

Some other young men were sitting on a patch of grass and called out to bet the others that they wouldn't have the stamina to sit on their horses through the whole show, sooner or later they would need to dismount to pick up a woman or urinate, or would simply drop down drunk to the ground.

'I don't reckon so. You can do anything on horseback – piss and pick up women.'

Then they started recounting adventures they claimed to have had, in which they were always on horseback. In coarse and long-winded accounts they sank into wetsands and quicksands, struggled their way out of the mire or were almost sucked down to hell. The people lying stretched out on the ground rolled around with laughter at these obviously fictitious feats and tribulations, while the ones on horseback shook with self-contentment. But a shiver and a sensation of wonder passed through the girl when she imagined allowing herself to be sucked down into quicksand and the weird fish that hid away there bit her toe with its poisonous teeth.

Snooty older men walked past the young ones, with the demeanour and expression of people of stature who own land, animals, grown-up children and plenty of hay. Security, assets and sheds full of cattle radiated from their faces. They were also well past the age when they had seriously stopped approaching women with insistent potency, but did so rather with their impotency and in trite submission.

The girl headed after them. No matter where they went, the conversation immediately turned to animals and they were constantly saying 'good day' and 'nice to see you again'. Somewhere she none the less lost track of them, but then she recognized the actor who had performed an excerpt of some play or other and had pulled extraordinary faces, so she pursued him instead. Now he was walking around the showground like an ordinary person, seemed to know almost everybody, and wore a permanent open-mouthed smile on his face. He had joined up with a fat couple who were supposed to read out poems in tribute to men and women up on a platform between two flags.

In front of them rode two men on stallions, with fluttering flags. They held the flagpoles some way out in front of themselves with their right hands, and supported them by resting the ends against the toe caps of their riding boots. Everyone thought this was typically Icelandic and solemn, but someone said it was obvious that the farmers didn't suffer from corns if they could put up with the weight of the flagpoles on their toes.

'The good old Icelandic custom of paying tribute to the womenfolk must never be lost,' said the actor, and his open-mouthed smile went wide open.

He could hardly make his way across the showground. People were always stopping him, many said they had seen him somewhere and then he would say very gently, 'that's more than likely,' but if they claimed to have seen him on television he would ask 'when?' as if he were either such a permanent fixture on the screen that he had lost track of his appearances, or so modest that he had completely forgotten whether he had ever been on television at all. This made him seem extremely amicable.

A woman thanked him wholeheartedly for all his roles in all his stage performances, and then he said, 'I have a dream. Ever since I was a child I've longed to own a chalet in this beautiful place here in such a flourishing rural district.'

To explain his longing he added that he had spent the summers on a local farm as a child, with his feet permanently wet from the marshland, but that had done no harm to him or his health – 'I'm as fit as two pins' – and perhaps he would buy something, perhaps a suitably sized plot of land for a little chalet where he could pop in and rest and wind down from the stress, if they could manage to engage him to produce a good piece of drama at the local community centre.

'Yes, it would be a great encouragement for the amateur theatrical group if someone with experience directed a production for the next local arts festival,' the woman said. 'We've no dramatic training whatsoever.'

'But you have the love of acting,' the actor said. 'That's the vital thing, in professional theatre too.'

'We haven't even got enough of that,' the woman said with an embarrassed smile. 'You can never give people a shout to meet up together any more, they're all so alienated, even in the countryside.'

'That's bad,' said the actor, 'but it can be rectified by voice training.'

The girl could hardly hear the conversation, because the Swans brass band had started playing and the vicar had gone up on to the platform. He drummed together the tips of his outstretched fingers.

His wife had finished reading patriotic poems. Her face was flushed, and when she saw the actor she sent her regards to the Director of the National Theatre.

'You're with him, aren't you?' she asked. 'His wife and I stayed at the same farm, we both hailed from Reykjavík but I stayed put underneath the cows and I don't have the slightest regret about turning old and grey there.'

She laughed and added, 'Your actors' wives must be a huge support to you.'

'A hundred per cent,' the actor replied.

Noticing suddenly that the girl had been following him around for a long time, he turned sharply and gave her such a look that she backed off.

By the time the day had worn on and the athletics were over, most of the people were drunk. Then they started shouting and calling out to the actor, 'Do some impersonations for us.'

The landowners stood upright in groups beside the white heads of the flagpoles and suggested by what they said that they could withstand anything at all, even though all the others were rolling around and slurring their words. The flags fluttered above their heads, because beneath them they opted for serious discussions of the problems of the country and nation. The actor greeted the gentlemen farmers as his equals on the stage, but they hardly waved their huge hands in the slightest in his direction while the noisy, clamorous words poured out of their mouths and the wet flags slapped together occasionally in sharp gusts of wind.

The brass band started playing on the platform again. The musicians were dressed in blue uniforms and wearing white caps with black peaks and badges with shields on them. There was a white swan swimming on the shields against a blue background with a white edge, which was supposed to represent water or sea. All the tunes the band played were light marches, even though most of the guests could no longer stand on their feet properly, apart from some of the older women.

Suddenly the brass band was gone. It seemed to have vanished into thin air. The platform was empty for a while. A shower started and the timber shone white in the dampness. Then the weather cleared up, the sun shone on the platform and the water rippled away in light clouds of steam, leaving dry patches behind. Afterwards the dance band took the stage and started playing.

The girl wandered up above the showground, planning to hide somewhere for the rest of the day until people starting thinking about going back home, but she could not find an unoccupied space anywhere. In virtually every grassy hollow there was a man lying on top of a woman to protect her from the shower. The men had their trousers down and their backsides shone bare and white. When the girl walked past one of the hollows, a man who was keeping a woman covered up doffed his cap and bowed his head to her, without moving from the woman who screeched, 'Who are you saying hello to while in the middle of this?'

'Good day, my girl,' the man said solemnly and calmly, without answering the woman.

The woman swung her head around, gave a curious look at the girl and called out, panting for breath, 'You ought to be ashamed of yourself, you filthy thing. At your age, staring at the grown-ups when they're on the job? Bugger off.'

On saying this she jerked her head, laughed, bandied her arms about and stuck her tongue out between her lips and wagged it in the face of the man, who arched his neck and head, doffed his cap and waved it in the air, and delivered a succession of greetings to the girl, who had been standing frozen to the spot watching them, but then backed off to the top of a hillock. When she came back down and looked down the hillside to admire the view, she saw the entire Swans brass band spread far and wide in their white shirts on top of women on the slopes, protecting them from the shower; the musicians had their blue trousers pulled down and their backsides shone bare. Beside each one lay the shiny instrument that he had been blowing into with all his might on the platform earlier in the day. None of them had taken off his peaked cap. The girl spent a long time watching the writhing hillside in the rain. When she had been contemplating the band for quite a while, a musician stood up as if rising from a nest, with his pants around his ankles: He grabbed his polished and shiny horn that was glittering now, because the weather had cleared up, and blew it so sharply and loudly that the girl was struck by a noisy slap of air on the cheeks. She retreated, afraid, and ran away. As she ran she vaguely noticed other men rising up from their women at this, because there was bright sunshine now and they did not need to lie on top of them; the sun glittered on the bare women in their undignified positions. When the girl was definitely out of their sight she could hear the blaring of brass behind her from every hollow, so loud that she thought the players were walking slowly, menacingly, after her with their trousers hitched up, in white shirts with the tails hanging out, thrusting silvery horns to their mouths between their inflated cheeks. But when she dared to look back she saw nothing but the white clouds above the hill and the newly washed blue of the sky. Then she sat down panting in a hollow where no one else was lying and caught her breath, holding her fingers over her mouth.

All of a sudden an elderly farmer had come over to her and started looking her up and down. Having done so, he asked, 'Are you from somewhere local?'

'No.'

'Then you're from the city.'

'Yes.'

'Well, I can see you're too young to be hanging around in the grass.' He groaned and darted his eyes at her.

'It's not healthy for girls to go looking for berries before the berries have turned blue and ripe and in full bloom and the basket is ready to put them in,' he said. 'But I was just looking for my people to invite them for some coffee.'

Then he asked how old she was.

'Nine.'

'Well, then we should just have ourselves some coffee, old style,' he said after taking a long look at her. 'But it's not because I don't fancy green berries and all that.'

103

The sun was shining so brightly that he squinted, and he started asking her about his people, as if she knew them, because they were all lost.

'Have you seen them? My old woman's easy to recognize.'

'No,' she answered. 'Only the people in the brass band.'

'Yes, anyone with a shiny polished horn can do what the hell he likes and give the kiss of life to the living dead,' he said.

As soon as he finished the sentence the air around her in the hollow grew warmer. She did not dare to leave and he kept looking at her.

'I'll show you the brass band,' she said.

'Take this old codger and drag him to his feet then,' he asked.

Instantly, everything turned into a game. He grunted with pleasure when she tugged at him, laughing. He did not release his grip on her afterwards and they walked hand in hand in the direction of the showground. The man walked ponderously and she hopped full of life on the tussocks around him, without wanting to let go of his grasp; he had exceptionally long arms, so she could jump around some distance from him. People started looking at them because they were coming from the opposite direction from the showground. A young girl was strolling with a young man not far from where they had been sitting, and she ran straight over to the old man.

'This is my daughter,' he told the girl gently, a vague smile playing across his lips. 'That couple aren't holding hands like us.'

'Where have you been hiding?' his daughter asked as if she'd been looking for him.

The lad had walked away suddenly as if the girl were nothing to do with him.

'Where?' asked the old man. 'Don't you suppose we've been out in the grass like everyone else?'

'I mean you and Mother,' the girl said.

'Your mother's lost and gone to the trolls, and I got lost too even though I know this place.'

The daughter smiled, not believing him, and said mockingly, 'You'd just love to get yourself lost, you old codger, but you're too old to get lost properly. You don't get lost in the night, to say nothing of here in the middle of the day with loads of people around.'

Then she supported the old man by the arm and led him along by her side. For a while the girl dragged along with them, reined by his arm, then he released his grip on her. She walked slightly hesitantly and hurt after them, but soon felt she was out of all contact with the show again, even though there was bright sunshine and she had bumped into a kind-hearted old man.

18

The dance had started on the platform where earlier the poems of tribute to women had been delivered and the brass band had played marches. People were constantly storming on to it, slobbering rather than embracing, to take a few peculiar steps there and swing themselves back and forth with great commotion, but they did not seem to stay on stage for very long afterwards. This applied mainly to the young people. If a male asked a female up to the platform, they would take a few tottering dance steps and she would wriggle her shoulders, throwing her head around as if deranged and not knowing whether to rest her cheek against his shoulder, or which one. Before she had made up her mind they had gone back down again anyway and disappeared out into the grass. On the other hand, there were always a few plump women dancing with each other on the same spot in one corner, and some of the older people never left. They seemed to be dancing in the same steps and positions, but would jerk their heads to the left to glance at the ones who were leaving or crane them to the right to watch them go out past the platform. Among the dancers were a middle-aged man and woman, both extremely well dressed, neat and perfumed in loose-fitting clothes and doing an endless artistic dance, according to what the girl heard people around her say up against the fence enclosing the platform, 'Those people come here to dance artistically, not to hook anything.'

The woman glided forwards in a white dress whose width and style matched the broad but rigid smile on her lips. The man soared lightly holding her in his arms, in between the momentary pauses they took to look into each other's eyes before he thrust one knee and then the other between her legs, according to the way they changed rhythm, and swung her backwards so that she opened her mouth even wider and seemed to swallow a few raindrops. Then he pulled her softly back upright, while she lay as if in her death throes on the black sleeve of his dinner jacket. But then she woke slowly, with a tender smile, from her trance of ecstatic delight, her eyes glittering in a silent thrill at the prospect of life, and they danced their artistic dance the whole day long and never once popped out into the grass. They didn't even slip out to the coffee marquee for a moment during the short showers, to get themselves some refreshments, warm up or bump into acquaintances and say, 'It's been ages since we've met.'

After people had said that they would discuss how they should all meet up much more often, it did everyone good to renew old acquaintanceships and maybe meet regularly a few times a year; people in the same district and even neighbours hardly know each other these days.

The women sat by themselves at a long table, chattering away and saying that they too should set up a local children's playground, and that there ought to be a day-care centre, hairdresser's salon and yoga centre for tired housewives to keep fit, women ought to throw their cars straight into the nearest mudpool, the best thing for country people would be to have a trained instructor who could teach them to jog between the farms, there was plenty of nature to do it in, that was the way for the womenfolk in particular to get themselves up and moving.

'You old yokel women rather ought to get in some training about how to become old maids again!' a drunken man called out.

The women roared with laughter.

'Well, thank God they're still around, drunken men of the old school with mouths that never close,' they said.

The girl had sat down at an empty long table and got herself some coffee. On a chair at the table beside her sat a drunken man. He was middle-aged and had been sitting there for a long time, and people avoided him or shied away because he would burst out in a rage every so often, make a noise and act differently from everyone else. If he addressed or talked to one of the coffee-drinkers, he soon started spouting nonsense or ramblings whose meaning no one could fathom. When the girl moved over to sit beside him – there was a suitable interval between them and the others and very few people remained in the tent despite the incessant rain that beat down on it at that moment with a soft, soporific rumbling – he suddenly took off his jacket and rolled up his shirt-sleeves.

'Look,' he said, and showed her his right forearm on which there were deep cracks and peeled skin which was red and covered with pus.

'Do you know what that is?' he asked and pressed close to her with his forehead, so that she smelt the alcohol on his breath.

He seemed to find it more difficult to breathe after pressing his forehead against her, and succumbed to a heavy, comfortable and provocative sleep. The man himself was heavy, big-limbed and large, although he was bony. Now he lost the power of speech and air came out of his chest with a sucking action, not unlike a constricted, turbulent wave which crashes upwards in foaming splashes between big boulders on the shore.

'No,' the girl answered at last. 'I don't know what that is.'

'The sun,' he said wearily up against her ear. 'That's what's eaten my arms away. I've had them bare all summer and that space cannibal was trying to devour my flesh with its greedy rays. Those are the forks it dips into my cooked meat.'

The man pulled a face and grew pensive.

The girl looked at him out of the corner of her eye, then examined the swollen flesh on his forearm, which was brown, curved, slightly hairy and dirty. He thrust his hand into her face.

'Look, my dear little girl,' he said. 'The sun pricked me with the prongs of all its forks.'

The girl looked at the arm, wishing that the man would take a tight, quick grip of her head with his other hand, which would surely have covered the whole of her skull with its fingers reaching down to her ears, and would smother her mouth and nose deep into the wrinkled, sunburnt flesh, so that, unable to breathe, she would sink her teeth into the sores and the pus would gush between her teeth like yellow fat. She was startled at this unexpected yearning, felt a nauseous discomfort in her stomach and was on the verge of being sick, but at the same moment her mind soared out into a dusky cranny where there was delight and a comfortable warmth which smelt of sweet-and-sour wine and an empty stomach. She stood up.

'Don't leave me,' the man pleaded, and grabbed loosely for her. 'I'll tell you some more about the sun.'

Even more people had left the tent and by now they were sitting alone at the long table. On it was a white cloth stained with coffee. In some places it had shifted and was crumpled from the man's arms, and it had folded over to reveal the shabby table underneath. Almost everyone had gone, only a couple of men and women were standing in a group and laughing by the entrance, bathed in yellow light, because at that moment the sun was shining on the corner and made the canvas translucent, casting a yellow glow over them. The long table next to them was piled with dirty plates with cutlery and cups on them. A few napkins had fallen on to the floor and been trampled into the grass.

Panting for breath, the man started telling the girl an incomprehensible, disjointed and sentimental story about the sun while he leaned forward on to the cloth-covered table, so obsessed with his subject that he did not even look at her any more. So she slipped away, picked the napkins up from the ground and folded them into a paper bird. The afternoon sun waned and gradually disappeared from the roof of the tent. The girl sensed the time, that it was late in the day and doubtless time to go over to the paddock, rein up the horse and wait for the people from the farm. But then the man grabbed her and she let him hold her tight when the sun slowly slid off the top of the tent and a warm darkness spread over them, bringing everything out of exalted brightness and back to earth. It grew dusky inside and became cold, while the moist scent of grass trampled by countless feet wafted up. This made the tables merely dirty tables and the plates ordinary dirty plates.

The women came out from behind the sheet, huddled together in noisy talk and started to collect all the rubbish from the tables and dash the cloths off them, so that what the girl had felt to be splendid and solemn before was unveiled in an instant as wretched and naked.

'I'll tell you for ever about the sun that eats men's flesh,' the man said, but clearly had nothing left to say.

It was as if he were too short of breath to continue talking or pumping out the words at her with his lungs. The two of them sat like that at the last table which had a white cloth on it, and he rested his clenched fist several times against his mouth.

From where the girl was sitting she could see out of the door of the tent. A new shower had started and the grass outside the entrance absorbed its dampness. The footprints in the mud there filled up with water. Then the sun returned. Now it only managed to shine on to the very top of the yellowish tent roof, but this was still enough to fill it once again with soft light.

Suddenly the man let go of her. She moved cautiously away from him and left. Yet she kept peeping inside and the last thing she saw was him sitting alone while the woman at the entrance counted the notes, smoothed them out and placed them in two shoeboxes, weighting the wad down with a stone.

The girl crept away from the marquee at a snail's pace so that she could see right inside it even from farther off. The women had started arranging the tables that emerged beneath the cloths. Now the man was sitting at a bare long table, pressing his clenched fist to his temple and watching her leave, or at least she thought so.

When she reached the paddock she felt how the fear of the summer and the yearning and vague sense of being unwell, which had constantly ambushed her, vanished from her body if she thought about the deranged and stocky man with his sunburnt arm. So she mentally sank her teeth into it and decided to keep her mind fixed on his swollen arm for the sole purpose of being able to let her fear loose on him, by taking a hard bite into those ruddy, unhealable sores.

19

A large number of people rode off from the meeting together; at first there was a large, sprawling group of wobbly men and noisy women who laughed at each other and bandied teasing remarks, riding on their noble steeds. But as soon as they reached the first crossroads their ranks began to thin and people went their separate ways. This went on at each crossroads. Gradually whole groups or individual riders left the caravanserai for the farms.

Several cars drove past them and beeped their horns to try to frighten the horses. Generally these were young people from outside the district. Few farmers had gone there in their cars, except to give a lift to the older people, who had been driven home after they had discharged their duties and the day had worn on. After that the farmers returned, this time riding their horses. Through their loyalty to the horse, country people wanted to show that they were still true farmers, independent of mechanized vehicles and instinctively attached to their pedigree steeds. To underline the point still further they took snuff, but it made them sneeze, since they had grown unaccustomed to it and their upper lips turned brown and they looked idiotic. Young men never took snuff except at the country shows, but their numbers were steadily dwindling too.

'There's nothing typically Icelandic about taking snuff, it's just messy,' they said.

Most of the riding party on the way back were drunk but tried to sit their horses with dignity all the same. On the way they laughed and sang patriotic and rural songs, but the poems on people's lips rarely got past the middle of the song, after which only the tune was heard and the words were replaced by a blaring *tra-la*. Patriotic songs had long become threadbare in people's memories, in spite of the fact that even the young people were eager to hum along to them when they were drunk. Yet there always was someone who knew them off pat and would lead the singing. Then the others would resort to the clever ruse of trailing slightly behind, lagging sufficiently to be able to learn the lines from the leader's lips yet singing fast enough to stay in key, thereby giving the impression that they knew the words.

Such charades were becoming a thing of the past now, too. Young people were so free they would admit unashamedly that they did not know the words any more and did not care either. Deep down inside they felt, none the less, that it was their duty to know the sentimental patriotic songs and sing them at the country shows, but because these were held only once a year it was not worth learning them. People couldn't be bothered. And, what's more, no one could remember the following day whether the others knew them or not anyway, whether they'd sung snatches of the words or hummed along, because everyone was drunk and no one pretended to remember anything that might be worse and more uncomfortable than not knowing the words to patriotic songs. They would be delivered in snatches, but as the song progressed the groups started humming along with great relief and joy. Anyone who tried to seize the opportunity to sing in English was quickly hushed down.

The women tutted about the snuff too and could not understand what it was supposed to mean, sniffing it up your nose like that. They smoked cigarettes on horseback and said they were no less worthy for doing that. They also drank straight out of the bottle like men and had bags of beer bottles by their saddles or held beer cans in one hand. They didn't want to be inferior to the men in any respect. As the party rode on they gradually gathered into a separate women's group and continued to discuss where the local women should meet up and set up an association that was for women only, and one of them said, 'This district ought to have the strength of character to bring in a genuine qualified judo instructor from Japan.'

The group welcomed the idea and rode in a tight cluster to be able to drink a toast to the suggestion. Then they started trying to remember how many economics graduates there were among the farmers in the district; there were several, most of them running mixed-production farms. The women were surprised at how many there were, and likewise that there were no qualified pre-school teachers in the district.

'That's the way we women are treated,' they said, unable to accept that there was no qualified educationalist to manage the proposed playground.

Men and women alike who hail from these parts but study medicine or nursing move to the city, but the economists return to the farms of their fathers.

That's an odd trend in the wrong direction.

'Maybe we country folk are still so healthy we don't need medical help or nursing!' one of them said, and they all drank a toast to it.

But we've got a woman vicar.

The women were unanimous that they wanted to live comfortable, healthy lives, so that the countryside would be a fair match for the city as far as keeping fit was concerned.

'We can drive the kids to the playground in the mornings then meet up to read each other's fortunes with Tarot cards,' one of them said.

They drank a toast to that, straight out of the bottle.

They seemed poised to write down on the spot a whole timetable for what they were going to do in the future: play cards, learn handicrafts, go to drawing classes, study dramatic expression and undergo group awareness training under the guidance of a group awareness instructor once a week.

We're completely lacking in group awareness in this district, and in body language too.

Then they left the group with their husbands or made their way off home to their farms, resolved to meet over coffee more often, dump the kids, get roaring drunk, act like incorrigible male chauvinists, tell endless dirty stories and taste each other's baking. They swore an oath to hold a joke women's liberation meeting under the slogan 'The South Iceland Women's Baking Commune', where each of them would improvise bread or make cakes on a whim.

At this, they rolled around laughing about how distinctive female humour was – 'It's a joke all to itself.'

Optimism prevailed among both sexes. The farmers discussed their own issues, too. They were most taken with the prospect of setting up a company for the direct marketing of products from their own potatoes, Icelandic red.

Someone said he had had the idea for a long time of setting up a little factory to produce a special type of chip for the domestic market, salted crisps, roast potatoes for the Sunday joint and sweet potatoes for dessert, and not least to experiment with stuffed potatoes with exotic flavours, similar to the ones he had eaten on the Farmers' Union trip abroad when they went to Singapore for a laugh to shake off the midwinter gloom and look at the transsexuals, and all came home appalled that such things should exist in the world, although it was only natural to try them out – 'But the difference depends upon how you look at it.'

'It's a simple matter of creating a marketable product from Icelandic potatoes,' he said. 'And surely a lot more people than just transsexuals could be persuaded to eat it.'

'And why not produce dried mash potato and compete with the Swiss?' one of them asked sarcastically.

Their conversation grew empty, sarcastic and disjointed as the party gradually thinned out. People turned gloomier, their optimism and the effect of the alcohol wore off and they felt the vast hopelessness that was the main thing this little nation had cultivated in its little land, and in fact the only thing it had to offer on any great scale. Before they reached their destination they said with sobs but wry smiles that not even Icelandic potatoes could take on the world except by wishful thinking, even though none in the world could match them for taste, wholesomeness and quality.

'Everything here is best, but no one out in the big wide world knows that, because the bounties of the earth carry no threat, no war or atom bombs,' one of them said. 'Kill people like they did in the Sagas and you'll capture global attention.'

Ahead of them, directly above the road, was a small, grey and heavy cloud, full to bursting with rain, and when the remainder of the party rode under it a downpour broke which would have drenched them all to the bone if they hadn't been stirred to action and galloped off apace to avoid the torrent. Most of the rain landed on the road, and when they looked back there was no cloud, but from the wet patch on the ground they could tell the shape it had been in the sky.

It was approaching midnight but the sun started shining again, a weak flash of dull gold.

The farmers from the cluster of farms rode to their respective houses on their respective hills. The cows had come out to the edge of the meadow and hung around by the gate, clearly tired of waiting for someone to milk them, because when they saw the people they began to moo with hoarse, pained sounds. They stood in three rows and lifted their heads almost in unison, stretched them forwards in a huge arc in the direction of their masters and gave deep, prolonged moos. There was a gloomy accusation in their bellowing.

While they acted aggressively the girl felt they were changing into enormous dogs with swollen udders and stiff teats. She thought it more natural for dogs to welcome humans by barking than for cows to reprimand their masters by mooing. Once she had changed her clothes she was sent down to the meadow to round them up into the cowshed. They swung their tails, clumsy and obstinate, snorting disdainfully, as if they were making up their minds whether they ought to milk in drops this time around, in revenge for having been made to wait well into the night.

As soon as they started to be milked everything returned to the way it had been before the country show. The show had vanished into the remote distance and the day was even farther away than the one which had been yesterday, and the girl felt how the remote past can be closer in the mind than that which has only just gone by. The same went for the distance. She closed her eyes for an instant to rid herself of it and wish herself away. Her mind set off into the paddock where the German girl was making horses rear up and wave their front legs like four-legged spiders. But when she reopened her eyes her body was in the same place it had been before she closed them. It was in the cowshed with the cows which snorted and sniffed with deep breaths. She saw the milk writhing out of them to meander along the milking tubes, the way it jerkily and unwillingly proceeded from its rightful place in the udder and into the refrigeration tank. It appeared to prefer being in the cows rather than in the round refrigeration pot, but through the volition of others it was not allowed to be where it belonged. Nothing is allowed to be in its proper place. If everything were allowed to stay in its place indefinitely it would stagnate and die.

The girl watched the trickling milk in the tubes and sensed her kinship with everything. Everything slipped into her mind, entwined in melancholy. On the other hand, the cows seemed happy and relieved at having got rid of the milk, because when they had been milked they lay down groaning with pleasure in the stalls and began to ruminate meaningfully. Then the farmer came in and asked, 'Do you know anything about the farmhand?'

'No,' she answered in surprise and remembered having seen him now and again, wandering around at the show, and that he had set off home with them but probably not made it back for some reason.

'Then we'll have to go and look for him,' said the farmer.

'Me?' the girl asked in surprise.

'I suppose you can come with us if you want,' he replied.

20

The horses were found just outside the wall of the meadow, the farmer and his daughter quickly mounted them and the girl decided to ride after them too on the mare and look for the farmhand. She was last, and the daughter rode in front.

It was a shadowy night and a calm dusk lay over everything, but the girl managed to keep her eye on where the farmer and his daughter were riding. They took a shortcut, went along the riverbank to the estuary, while she rode along the road. When they reached the estuary a number of swans were taking off and sang that disconcertingly beautiful song that swans sing when autumn is approaching and they fly off into the shadowy night. The girl stopped her horse to watch them leave, the way they seemed to take to the air with great effort, then glide unearthly and rejoicing out into the green brightness until they vanished and could be heard no longer.

While she was waiting on her horse, the yearning for night came over her, a strong longing and wish that such light would always reign, that there were neither day nor night in the world, but instead twilight outside and indoors and within her too. The thought struck her that the farmhand must be dead, he would have merged into the dusk clutching his diaries. He had taken them with him to the country show to be able to prove his worth by them, if he were lucky enough to find himself a sweetheart and prospective lifelong companion at last. At that moment it seemed just as if he were everywhere around her in the same way as people who have recently died and her grandmother. He was also inside the horse she was sitting on, because the sensation of him permeated her from the warmth of its back.

Then she wished she had chanced upon the wishing hour and been turned to stone while the world stood still, in the same kind of light at midnight, but for all she could see the daughter and the farmer were driving a horse along in front of them with a pile or bundle on its back.

She had lost sight of the farmhand at the country show early in the day, he had been roaming around endlessly, popped up or disappeared just as quickly as all the other people. But she saw him going around with the daughter and he looked puffy-cheeked and distracted.

'Men like that have no place in existence and never will, however intelligent and hard-working they might be,' she heard the farmer say to someone, but did not know whether he was referring to the farmhand. And he added, 'So, he's one of those old bores who can't take a drop of drink without crying his eyes out. And not for any understandable reason.'

At these words the farmhand turned into a raincloud in her mind, a man who belonged in the guise of rain and never stopped pouring except for a few moments when he sat down at the table in his room in the evenings to write in his diary the affairs of his heart and what he had done that day. He could not have poured tears into it, that would have wiped out what he wrote, but perhaps everything he wrote with ink was dry tears. Her curiosity awakened and she decided to sneak a look at the diary the next morning to find out what had happened to him at the show; she knew where he kept it.

While she was thinking this, the farmer and his daughter brought a heap on horseback up to the riding track alongside the ditch. There were a few clouds in the sky and they reflected in the shadowy water which was brighter than the surrounding air; it absorbed the hints of brightness from the sky and magnified them enchantingly on its calm surface where buttercups grew and stretched themselves out of it on tall sallow stalks, spreading their green waxy leaves. The contemplative air of calmness about the plants, and the secrets of the bottom which was deep down inside the porous ground, made the water greater and heavier than any other water.

A small amount of traffic was still on the road, mainly jeeps.

Drunken youngsters from distant districts called out through the open windows and laughed, and a squeaky voice asked, 'What's that bag of rubbish on your horse?'

'It's not a bag of rubbish, it's a misery bag,' answered an equally squeaky and jolly voice.

Then an empty bottle was thrown into the ditchwater and the car zoomed off, its tyres screeching against the road.

At almost the same instant the pile on the horse's back began to stir and whimper. At first it was a low mumble, then it turned into a loud wail which made the horse stop in its tracks, arch its neck and head and cock its ears, as if considering itself under threat and trying to work out where it was coming from by pointing its ears quickly in all directions.

The farmer and his daughter had come so close to the girl that she could see it was the farmhand. He was slumped over the front of the horse with his head buried in its mane, just as she had done when she became separated from the rest of the party on the road, but he seemed to be paralysed or sapped of strength.

'Pull yourself together and act like a man!' the daughter called out. 'You're making a fool of yourself.'

'I don't give a damn about anything,' the farmhand muttered.

'There, there,' the farmer said.

The girl did not know whether the farmer was asking his daughter to stop, or the farmhand, who seemed to calm down on exchanging words with other people, but still lay forward over the horse's neck.

'Sit up straight,' the farmer said firmly. 'It's over and done with now. Please, for my sake . . . as usual.'

The farmhand straightened himself up slightly, but at the same moment a car drove along the road and someone called over to the daughter, who rode up to it and stayed on horseback while she talked to the people inside. They leaned out through the window and looked at the farmhand, who slumped forward again.

'A noble figure as usual, that farmhand!' someone called out of the car. 'He's in the same state he gets in every summer.'

The farmer did not reply. He sat still on his restless horse and the night became embarrassing, even the glow from the sky, everything but the wakeful flowers that peeped up through the surface of the water. Even the girl wanted to sink down into the ground but also was eager to find out how it would end, because she'd never seen anything like it before although she knew she was witnessing a tragedy that befalls men in such light, when it is neither day nor night, neither dark nor bright, neither good nor bad, but some humiliation takes place. On this intuition she began crying too. The people in the car saw this and someone said, not loudly, but the voice carried over to them in the stillness, 'You seem to have got a few sprinklers around you this exceptionally sunny and dry summer. May the tears do your daughter good.'

The young people in the car waved to her when they drove away slowly so that she would move out of the way and not get run over.

The daughter was seized by a fury, she swung away impulsively from the car, dug her spurs into the horse and stormed at the horse with the bundle on it, which did not know whether it was allowed to move out of consideration for the tragedy in the mind of the man hanging on its back. When the daughter came charging up with her whip aloft, the horses crashed into each other. The one with the farmhand on was unprepared for the assault and leapt off the road. In doing so it lost its balance and slammed on its side into a mudpool. The surface of the water split open into countless black mirrors. It smoothed out facing the sky into sharp-pointed arrows and grew choppy at the sides in tight waves of light and black. The horse snorted louder, tried to rise to its feet, to jerk itself up out from the shallow mire, and it stretched out its neck and held its head high but seemed to have become stuck to the mud, unable to get to its feet which flailed around uncontrollably. The farmhand had landed underneath it. The girl could not see him for all the splashing. The twirls, spasms, kicking and futility of the legs that tried to gain purchase in the air made her dazed, half hypnotized, and she wanted to throw herself into the water. Then suddenly the farmhand's hand emerged from beneath the horse and tried to grab hold of something in a similar fashion to the legs seeking a foothold.

'He'll drown there,' said the farmer.

Then, cursing him, he jumped out into the pool.

'Get out of here,' the daughter ordered the girl. 'Bugger off back home.'

And the moment she said this, she ran after her father.

They were soaked through to the skin at once, shied away from the horse's kicking and could not get to the man underneath it. Their clothes were drenched, almost the same black colour as the water and the marsh, but because they kept moving around the place where the splashing came from, the girl could follow what was happening. Eventually the farmer managed to get a grip on the horse's tail while the daughter moved in on it from the front and grabbed its mane, and soon afterwards they had pulled it to its feet. When it was standing up it raced off, without a moment's hesitation, at a tangent across the drainage ditches with its head to one side, because its bridle was hanging loose, and splashing and slurping noises came from under its hoofs.

'Get it, stop it!' the farmer called to the girl.

She obeyed at once and jumped out into the marshland too, although she knew she would never catch the horse.

Over the land lay the calm of night and the inviolable twilit brightness of late-summer unreality. When the girl stopped, already wet and smeared with mud, she looked over towards the farmer and his daughter who had managed to retrieve the farmhand from the water and drag him across the ditch with the buttercups in it and up on to the bank by the main road where the horses were standing still and waiting for them. Neither said a word. The farmer was about to lift the farmhand up on to his horse, but the daughter said firmly, 'I'll take him in front of me just this once.'

'Come on,' the farmer said archly. 'Don't you think you've done enough for one day?'

'I'll let him sit in front of me,' she replied slowly.

Together, they lifted the man on to the horse and he showed neither willingness nor resistance. Then they mounted their horses. They were all soaked through and silent.

When they set off in train past the girl she could hear the farmhand retching; he must have swallowed a lot of water and he threw up several times, and the daughter said, 'Now that drink ought to be wearing off a bit, or at least that stupidity of yours.'

She repeated this several times, but the farmhand just leaned back against her, exhausted and defenceless. He neither wept nor made any sound, he just lay helplessly up against the daughter who was soaking wet and covered with mud from the marshes, just like him.

The farmer got most of the water out of his clothes by brushing himself down hard with his palms before mounting. He cursed several times and was irritated.

'The time's come to put a stop to this,' he said.

He rode behind the others.

The girl stayed behind. A dull light played on the water around her and now she could see on the calm surface that a tiny dark cloud was sailing through the sky. She wanted to touch it with her foot, but when she stretched out and ruffled the water, the cloud vanished into the waves and merged with it. She felt it was too long to wait for the surface to settle down again, so she splashed her way out of the wetland and over the bank to the mare. Realizing that she could not ride along with the others on this occasion, she waited a long while and left them to themselves. She hung around there well into the night and hid by the roadside to prevent passing drivers from seeing her. The mare waited too, and did not move, even when beer cans were thrown at it from cars to try to frighten it .

When the girl woke up the next morning, slightly later than usual, and was going to check what the farmhand had written in his diary when he returned home, she could not find it where he always kept it under the big Bible. It had gone. And when she could not see him anywhere and cautiously enquired about him, the farmer's wife replied, 'He never came back from the show, so he's probably left this farm once and for all, God knows where to. Is there much chance he'll settle anywhere for long, the way things have gone?'

21

That morning the house was much emptier than on other days. It was easy to tell from the way everyone kept quiet. Something was missing. The farmer and his wife and their daughter were clearly on edge but kept themselves in check. None of them managed to do any useful jobs for most of the morning, so it was a welcome relief when the farmer said to his daughter, 'Well then, it's probably best for you to take the kids from the farms off on the annual trip up the mountain tomorrow; then that's over and done with.'

Towards lunchtime he sent the girl out to the marsh to fetch the mare, because he was going to shoe it. When she got to the horses the mare was nowhere to be seen; it had clearly bolted.

'We'll go over the river to get it,' said the farmer, when the girl returned to tell him the mare was not there.

'Me?' She asked in surprise.

'No,' he answered.

Now it seemed he had nothing more important to do than fuss about the mare.

'I'm not going with you this time,' the daughter replied. 'And you're not going in the car either, I need to use it,' she added firmly.

'Where are you going?' Her mother asked.

'My business.'

'Surely you're not starting again?'

'What's not over can never start again.'

'Bloody hell, that's some news,' the farmer said.

The daughter shrugged.

'Can't you use your own car?'

'It's broken down.'

The daughter looked at her father. His face looked shaken by storms and rains.

'You can come with me this once,' he said, addressing his words to the girl. 'We'll row over the river.'

'She's not strong enough to hold the animal by the reins,' the farmer's wife said. 'She's only a child.'

'Then the mare will pull us both into the river,' the farmer said disdainfully.

'Can't you possibly delay your plans until tomorrow?' the farmer's wife asked her daughter. 'Or fetch the mare in the car later today?'

The farmer stayed silent.

'I can go with you,' his wife said.

'What nonsense,' the farmer said, in a daze. 'The girl and I can handle the mare by ourselves.'

The girl followed him without him ordering her to. He went down to the river and she was right at his heels. The meadow had been mown and the hay gathered up, and the grass had turned yellow at the roots. The farmer started singing. He lifted his head as he walked and aimed his song across the river towards the opposite bank, the low slopes and the plain, the mountains beyond the plain and the hills where the farm stood out of sight, and doubtless the mare too, if it had got away by swimming over.

The girl started thinking about the water in the river and its colour, which was the white of skimmed milk, knowing that this was glacial water, melted glacier which flowed in a swirling current half-way between the banks.

They climbed into the boat without saying a word to each other. It creaked beneath their weight. It was an old skiff, battered and leaky, and the water in the keel was so deep that the girl's feet got wet.

'Start baling,' the farmer said in a neutral tone of voice.

He got back out of the boat to fetch the oars and secure the row-locks. The girl baled water out of the boat with a bent jug. The planks screeched discomfortingly when she dragged the jug along the bottom to reach all the water that had leaked in and pour it out into the still water which lapped against the sandy bank.

'That's enough,' the farmer said. 'Now sit down there on the rowing bench and keep still.'

She sat at the stern and he pushed the boat out, then hoisted himself up and clambered over the side. He did everything measuredly and did not sit down to row until the boat was well afloat and starting to turn around, as if it were trying to take the bearings of the current. It bobbed freely until the farmer put the oars out. The girl felt afraid, thinking the boat would drift out into the current which would snatch it away without the farmer being able to restrain it, and then he seemed to take ages fiddling around with the loose rowlocks and securing the oars. But he seemed to know the river, the boat and the current, and stayed calm even when the boat spun round in a circle for a while as he bent down to straighten up his boots. His bending over seemed to make the boat decide itself and set off. When it reached the point dividing the calm water from the current, and the rushing stream looked set to snatch it away, the farmer looked up, took his first few quick pulls on the oars and headed back for the still water alongside the bank. He rowed for a while, sitting with his face turned towards the girl, but instead of looking her in the face he stared out beyond or through her. He put his weight on the oars and came up to the place where the farmhand was accustomed to head straight out for the current.

All of a sudden he put down the right oar and pulled hard on the other, dipping its blade quickly but shallowly into the water, and the boat was hurled out into the current. After that he took deep strokes with the oars, rowing vigorously on both sides and exhaling with a rhythmical puff into a drawer that he produced with his mouth by projecting his lower lip.

The boat bounced around as though out of control, for all the farmer's furious rowing. He seemed to have something else on his mind or be listening to the water beneath the keel. Mentally sounding the depth, calculating his own force and comparing it with that of the current. The girl clutched tightly at the side of the boat. Then he looked at her for the first time and laughed.

'You'll drown anyway, whether you hold on or not, if we capsize,' he said.

She said nothing, but did not release her grip.

'Sit calmly, don't hold on,' the farmer said. 'Nothing can save us now if we end up in the water.'

The girl did not release her grip. The boat went on bucking and bumping down with a splash, cleaving the waves as if it were rushing over bumps on a hard road. The farmer said nothing else. His features creased as he worked the oars. By concentrating, he became the strain itself.

Before the girl knew it they had escaped from the swift current and reached the calm water close to the other bank. She felt relieved and her mind filled with rejoicing. It was still over that side, in the shelter of a high soil bank. She could smell the scent of moist grass, the pungent aroma of heather, and she wanted to get out of her boat prison at once and feel firm land under foot. Seeing this, the farmer laughed an understanding laugh, but said nothing. He laid to the bank slowly, paddling with the oars and continually looking over his shoulder to find the right place to go ashore. When he felt the boat grounding he got out of it, grasped the side firmly with one hand and pulled it effortlessly up on to the sand. The light, smoothed pebbles screeched beneath the keel.

'Out you come, miss,' he said. 'Have you wet yourself?'

'No,' she answered.

'Then you've got sea-legs.'

Then they walked up the hill along a narrow riding track, with him in front and her behind, and he started singing again; louder this time than on the other side of the river.

They walked for a long while across the hummocky ground off the track, because he took a shortcut, the earth was wet and difficult to cross but it gave off a lovely scent of plants which merged into the slopping of the water and slurping from beneath their boots. The farmer grew short of breath, stopped singing and started warbling. He was peculiarly jolly and looked at the girl from time to time, more cheerful than was his habit. In general he never looked at her back home, except when he ordered her to do some job. Yet he did not speak a word and they continued over dry knolls that stood up out of the wetland. On top of one of them he stopped, looked across the vastness for an instant and said, 'Oh!'

After that he continued on his way and they walked for long while until they reached a field, and the girl saw the mare standing grazing with other horses. The farmer pretended not to notice the horse that had bolted and she did not dare to point it out to him, because she had no right to point something out to him which he had overlooked, even if she could see better. They rounded a fairly long hill and then the farm came into sight.

The people there greeted the farmer, without stopping their work. They were rushing back and forth but went on conversing with him in snatches, forcing him to turn round in all directions and keep constantly on the move in order to address his words to the right people. The girl could tell he was losing his temper and was on the verge of turning back. It was obvious he felt he was being given a disgraceful reception. Maybe they thought it obsequious or unnecessary to come over at the beginning of the week, the day after the country show when there was plenty of work to be done. Besides which it was no great sign of good husbandry, not being able to keep the mare where it belonged or make it feel attached to him, even if it was only used as a pack-horse.

Just as he seemed about to say his farewell the woman stopped busying herself with her chores around the farm and said, 'Well, we've got a visitor.'

The farmer felt relieved and they went indoors, along with the other people on the farm. While he was waiting for coffee they enquired if his daughter was keeping well, which made him turn peculiarly still where he was sitting. He answered 'fine,' but changed the subject. They started talking about this and that until the conversation had lasted quite long enough. He stood up and took his leave.

The girl had not opened her mouth, and when they went back around the hill in the opposite direction and straight over to the group of horses, she remained silent. She looked in expectation at the mare which was grazing calmly without looking over at them. It did not even look up. They drew closer and the girl expected the mare to break into a run and give them a quick kick with its rear legs, to leave them lying covered in blood on the grass with their skulls smashed. The farmer walked up to the mare. It went on grazing, as if trying to bite as much grass in its home pastures as it could before being bridled and led away. And that is what it did. When the farmer was standing beside it, at last it lifted its head from the ground and he slipped the bridle swiftly around its mouth without saying a word, then led it away.

The mare offered no resistance, showed no reaction, and did not even drag at the reins.

The farmer, too, seemed not to care about the bother or effort it had caused him. He led it behind him along the same route, over the knolls, through the wetland and down to the river. This time he did not sing. The girl thought it strange that neither of them showed any sign of anger. She could not understand why the mare had bolted, if it had only been to have the farmer fetch it again and lead it like a lamb back to confinement. But she thought to herself that that was the way things were in the countryside, such was the relationship between men and animals.

'Well then,' said the farmer, who had led the mare out into the river.

The girl climbed aboard the boat.

'Take hold of the reins now; I'll row and you keep hold of it,' the farmer said, and launched the boat.

The girl took hold of the reins. The mare gazed into the air, twitched its ears and listened for something.

'Sit the other way round on the bench this time, like that, with your back towards me,' said the farmer, showing her how to sit tight. Press your foot against the side and hold on tight when the mare starts swimming. It gets rough then and the reins will suddenly jerk. Now you've got something else to do rather than be afraid. Do you understand?'

The girl did exactly as he had told her. She sat backwards in the boat, looking into the eyes of the mare which walked slowly on the long reins, following the boat as it moved away from the landing place. They were still in shallow water, but the river grew deeper and the mare lifted its head. They rowed alongside the bank.

'That's it,' said the farmer. 'Now give it all you've got.'

At that moment he swung the boat out into the current. The river suddenly deepened. The girl felt she was being tugged as the mare resisted sharply; it snorted, but plunged into the water with a splash. The girl held the reins with all her might. Although the mare was swimming furiously, its body sank slowly in the whitish water. Then it started snorting alarmingly, its eyes spread wide and terror shone from them.

The farmer acted as if nothing was happening. He went on rowing hard with the oars and puffing into the drawer of his lower lip.

The girl was convinced that the mare would sink to the bottom and drown. It was heavy and seemed unable to keep itself afloat for long in such a strong current. But the girl did not let go of the reins, even though she was certain the mare would flip her over the stern and pull her towards it. All the same, she was on the verge of letting go or calling out in terror, 'It's drowning.' Just then she chanced to look at the mare, which looked back with horror in its eyes and submerged helplessly even deeper into the water, as if it felt betrayed of everything, in the world of man and nature alike, so the best thing would be to take its own life. She felt deep sympathy for the mare, but at the same time hatred.

Then she looked anxiously over her shoulder at the farmer. He gave a cold laugh and she rolled her eyes back towards the mare. Now only its dark, spread and snorting nostrils stood up out of the water.

'Keep a bloody tight grip there, otherwise it'll pull you overboard,' the farmer hissed, prodding her with the toe of his boot to underline his words.

This gave the girl her power of speech back, and she groaned, 'It won't make it across, it'll drown.'

'Oh yes it will,' the farmer laughed teasingly. 'That animal won't kill itself, it's just spoilt and wants to be pitied.'

The girl gasped for breath.

'Animals do that too,' the farmer said. 'It can reach the bank on our side just as easily as its own bank on the other side. It's just as difficult a swim. If it were by itself and wanted to cross the river it would look after itself without any sympathy.'

A sense of calm came over the girl and she wanted to slip into sleep, she almost lost the power from her stiff legs which she pressed with all her might against the side of the boat to keep herself safe, but she also wanted to be dragged overboard and into the river to the mare, which would take her on its back at once and the two of them would swim for ages and ages down in the darkness in the cold day and night until they awoke one morning in the light of a new day and she would still be sitting calmly on its back and they would both have reached the endless ocean and dissolve into its waves and glowing sun.

But then they had reached the still water at the opposite bank. The farmer jumped straight out of the boat and tied it up. The mare stepped out of the river, glossy and extraordinarily beautiful, and he took the reins from it. It did not even glance back across the river to its youthful haunts, but just plodded away with heavy steps, having lost its hidden nature, its beauty, the need to die by its own instinct, and had become an ordinary, obedient pack-horse again. It roamed like this along the side of the fence around the meadow, back to the other group of horses, as if nothing had happened and it had never run away.

'Well, you can have the rest of the day off,' he said. 'Tomorrow's the biggest day of the summer.'

The girl stayed by the riverbank for a while, amusing herself with things there and thinking.

22

They had ridden in a more or less orderly group along the riverbanks, the bank of the big river and two smaller ones, then finally along the bank of the river that flowed in a wide meander past the mountain. On the way they passed the newly built stables where the horses were tamed. The German girl was sitting on a horse in the field in front of it. The children wanted to watch her taming them, but the daughter ordered them to keep together.

'Today we're on our way to the mountain, not to see a display of horse-breaking,' she said, adding that there was no point in going down to the stables anyway, it took a long time to train a horse.

In the field with the German girl was a young man who was attending to the horses. When the group stopped on the road he looked up instinctively, noticed the party and stared at them for a while. Then he put the reins on a horse and rode over the gravel bank between the field by the stables and the riverbank; it was a fair distance.

He greeted them before he had quite reached them. The girl recognized him immediately: he was the one she had seen at the country show accompanying the German girl, and had taken the girl's greeting so oddly that she remembered it, the way he swung his hand out casually, pretending to catch her greeting and clasp it in his palm.

This time they greeted each other in a different, more reserved fashion, but he was pleased to see the children.

'Well, the summer's drawing to an end then, since you're all here,' he said.

Then the two of them rode side by side along the riverbank until they reached a house. It was not large, with two storeys, but stood out because it was in a poor state of repair, the corrugated iron cladding had gone rusty in many places. It was a timber house, one of the few in the district. Most were built from stone these days. But the house had an air about it that no ordinary farmer lived there, maybe it was obvious from the dilapidated state it was in that he was resourceful enough not to maintain it but lived in an old shack instead.

They were welcomed by an elderly man. He was fairly stocky, not large, with a moustache and huge brown eyes. His voice was quite loud, but not shrill. Instead of greeting the children, he talked to them as if they'd always been at the farm.

'Say hello to Dad,' the young man said.

The children said hello to him and the girl could tell that this man was really too old to have a young son of the same age as the farmer's daughter. The man treated his son like those men who become fathers at a fairly advanced age and have children with much younger women. It was as if his son were his grandson, or just the mother's son. However, his birth had clearly been a stroke of serendipity which he scarcely believed could have happened at all, to say nothing of this coincidence reaching manhood. He was gentle in his manner towards the farmer's daughter. She seemed to be his daughter much more than his son was his son.

A middle-aged woman came out of the house. She asked the children to put their horses inside the paddock, then she greeted the farmer's daughter with a neutral disposition. The man wore an exalted expression at seeing her. She gave the clear impression that she was the wife and housewife. Before inviting them inside, she showed them a few flowers. The daughter looked at them without interest. She had never liked flowers and did not care in the least how difficult it had been to make them grow in this place. None the less, the woman was just as pleased. The man was pleased with the flowers too, because his young wife was.

The daughter told the children to stay outside and wait to be called indoors for refreshments.

'Yes, you just play outside,' the woman said.

Then the grown-ups went inside.

Everything in there was somehow in a state of organized decay, yet arranged according to the sense of order of certain faculties of the mind; the outhouses and the fences too. Nothing there was beautiful apart from the ornamental flowers which did not even grow in the garden but beneath the wall of the house. The girl could not figure this all out; she had heard the farm spoken of with respect, but when she saw the house she was not impressed at all. Only the man aroused a certain sense of reverence in her, but she did not know why.

The children ran around. She rushed about too, and could not decide whether she ought to go off somewhere by herself or join the other children and go up the mountain. They climbed up a few knolls with rock outcrops sticking out from them, but she grew bored with the game.

The mountain did not look as impressive or noble from there as it did from the farm where she was staying. The slopes were terribly ordinary slopes, covered with grass and not particularly steep. She couldn't even see all the way up it, not even up the peak. The sun was shining. She lay down for a while in a hollow at the foot of one of the knolls, then she walked over to the house, and decided not to go up the mountain. The man had come out by then, and since he was busily doing something for himself he did not notice her; or he did not care that she had turned up.

In the hallway was a steep staircase leading upstairs. The woman was talking housewife talk in the kitchen. The others were clearly drinking coffee.

'Yes, do help yourselves before I call the others in,' the woman said.

The girl resolved not to go into the kitchen, thinking she would disturb them. No one could see her, so she decided to take a closer look around the house and go upstairs. Expecting the stairs to creak, she slipped off her shoes and crept up slowly. The stairs did creak, but the people were doubtless so accustomed to hearing soft creaking in the house that it did not catch their attention. The woman in the kitchen did not lower her voice, the others said nothing but were surely listening to her rather more than to the creaking of the stairs.

When she reached the top there was a little corridor by the landing and the doors to four rooms were ajar. She went into each in turn; one contained only old things, another a large unmade old-fashioned bed. Everything in there was in a mess, but there were a lot of books. In the third room there was a large table in the middle of the floor with a computer that clashed with its surroundings. There was some writing on the monitor which she looked at but did not understand. It was a fairly small room, bright, with a comfortable armchair and a single flower on a table. Then she entered the fourth and largest room. It was half dark inside. When she looked to her right she saw a woman sitting there on a chair beside another unmade bed. Everything was old-fashioned and the bed was covered with quilts. It was the sort of room where for some reason you weren't allowed to touch anything. There was no way of telling how old the woman was, but she was probably as old as the hills, even though her smooth face did not show it. She was holding a big black comb, pondering it as it lay in her lap. When she looked up and saw the girl she groped instinctively towards her with the comb. The girl backed away, not from fear of the woman, but because she recalled her mother's words: 'Beware of the combs in the countryside, when I was there you could catch head lice from them.'

Although she knew this was nonsense, she took a couple of steps backwards all the same. Light entered the room through a large window, but the glazing was old and dimmed it. The old woman stretched the comb out at her again without speaking a word. Then she stroked her own hair, but the girl did not make a move. The woman's smile was static and warm. Judging from her features, she could have been the man's mother and the young man's grandmother. She had brown eyes, too, but bigger brows. She lifted the comb once more. Then the girl heard that the woman downstairs must have gone to the front door, because she called the children in to have some refreshments. The girl also heard the daughter and the young man, as he said, 'Let's nip out while the children are gorging themselves.'

Then suddenly it was obvious that they had gone upstairs. They could not be heard making any noise, because of the noise the children were making.

The woman stopped the arm holding the comb as if she were

listening for their footsteps, whether they could be heard coming from her room or from one of the others and, if so, from which one. But the footsteps did not approach. The young man whispered, 'It's all right, she's in a completely different world.'

The girl's heart started racing. Everything became so curiously quiet around her. She crept up to the door of the room she was in and peeped out into the corridor. The door to the room with the bed in was closed now. She tiptoed up to it, put her ear to it and heard the young man saying, 'I've missed you so much.'

The words were said in the hot tone of tragedy and loss which lies beyond tragedy, loss and weeping. The girl felt the current herself and the air grew sultry around her. From outside in the yard the clinking of horsebrasses or iron could be heard. The man went into the house and said something to his wife, who answered, 'They've gone out.'

The young man repeated his sentence in the same way, but the daughter said nothing; she stayed silent. After that came the sound of her fumbling with her clothes. Then he said, 'Not now; I'm too excited and it just won't work.'

'I don't care,' she said.

The young man continued to whisper things and heat up the air with his words, so the girl retreated to the old woman's room. As soon as she saw her the old woman lifted up the big comb. The girl was about to walk over to her and see what she wanted, but she didn't.

'Do you want to comb my hair?' she whispered.

The woman did not reply. The girl stood still watching the woman, who put the comb down in her lap and contemplated it carefully. Then the girl slipped back out into the corridor and listened at the door. Their whispering had stopped, and now they were talking in half-whispers the way people do when what is being hidden has already happened. Since it's just over and it's uncertain whether there were any witnesses, people talk in muted tones as a safety precaution, then the voices of the guilty acquire a normal pitch, and once it is certain that no one has heard anything they speak in unnaturally loud voices to assure conceivable witnesses that nothing at all has happened, no matter what they might think to the contrary. The girl had heard her parents doing a similar thing.

The daughter was speaking this time around, and the young man was silent.

The girl did not know what they were talking about. She could not pick up the thread; she'd spent too long in the old woman's room, giving them the chance to do what it was better for her to have in her mind than to have seen or heard or copied for herself with someone else, since she was only a child after all.

'Just listen for a moment . . .' the daughter said. 'No, not again . . . I've got one from him here.'

'No . . .' the young man whispered. 'Not now . . .'

'Yes, listen,' the daughter said firmly. 'His words are better than what you have to offer , . .. they get through to me better than that . . .' She fell silent. A short time passed. Then she made a sound as if she were smiling while she exhaled heavily through her nose. 'No . . .'

'Maybe,' he said, 'but the best for this is taking your time, and how you last . . .'

'I think anyone could die to hear a sentence like this,' she said. 'Then the one who could have died and wanted to doesn't, but rather the one who wants to live for his words and her . . .'

The young man said nothing. Their clothes could be heard rustling and they spoke at normal volume.

'Look,' she said. 'Just listen to this. And she seemed to be reading out: "Few things are better than when a hand touches a body, preferably the unfamiliar hand of someone, but you feel that the hand has always belonged in that place . . . where it touches you . . . That is not the hand that owns. Nor is it the hand that takes. It is the hand from the earliest of times . . ."'

The girl froze.

Neither of the others said anything.

'And what do you say to that?' the daughter asked.

'Yes, but it doesn't refer to love,' he said, 'not to physical love . . . nor to spiritual love.'

'What then?'

'Not to love for you or any living being; it's love for death.'

The daughter suddenly went silent. No sound could be heard from the room. The girl was shocked; she became afraid and rushed down the stairs. The woman came out of the kitchen and said, 'Oh, were you upstairs?'

The girl walked past her slowly. She made an effort not to give anything away.

'Aren't you going to have something to drink with the others?'

She did not answer. Something reminded her of its presence in her memory and she strolled across the meadow, went through the gate, and without even deciding to do so she had started to climb the mountain.

23

For the first part of the climb her mind carried her up there, past the hillocks that stood up out of the mountain, crowned with crags from the loose rocks that seemed to tumble gradually from them down on to the grassy slope. The crags looked like big black warts on the body of the mountain. She edged around them and continued on her way, even though she had no clear idea where she was heading because she had never been up the mountain before and did not know whether there was any particular route up the slopes, but she just hoped that she would hit upon the top if she kept on a straight course. She decided never to look back, not because she was superstitious and thought she would be turned to stone, but rather because of a suspicion that the landscape below, seen from high up on the slopes, would be so beautiful that she would make do with admiring it in the sunshine.

The weather was hot and she became a little tired from walking; she was wearing warm clothing, since they had planned to spend all day out riding and there was a chance that the weather would turn cold towards evening when the sun began to set, and you always feel chillier on horseback anyway. She took off some of her clothes. The grass was comfortable under her feet and she was surprised at how much growth there still was in it, how fertile the slope was even though it faced north and was surely beaten by the hard cold winds in winter. In occasional places, however, there were patches that had been eroded by the wind, where the brown earth and stony ground could be seen. She tried to edge her way around those places, after trying to take a shortcut across one of the patches of soil and so much mud had got stuck on her soles that it weighed her down when she walked, and it took her a long time to scrape the lumps from under her heels, which she had to do because otherwise her shoes were too slippery for walking on the grass.

By now she had climbed so high that she felt a slight fear of heights, not a genuine fear, but only if she imagined looking back and seeing that she had reached a vertiginous height. That made her feel cheerful.

She had walked for so long that she thought she must reach the top soon. But she didn't. She walked on for a while more and was thinking of giving up, sitting down and resting; the air around her was light and thin and gave the impression that it was late in the day, and if she were to sit down she would never get up again, but would fall asleep and neither make it to the peak nor back down again. At this thought a shiver ran through her, but it drove her onwards.

Suddenly the grass largely disappeared and was replaced by moss the green colour of angelica, then rocky gravel with no vegetation at all. Then she entered a low belt of fog which crawled, grey, along the ground, touching the rocks. She walked on like this for a short time, thinking to herself that the fog must be the same one that often curled around the mountain, a little way below the peak, and stretched out in a cloud from the bluff of the mountain and twirled down to the next river below, so she knew that she would soon leave it again and the sunlit peak would greet her. But when the fog cleared and the last grey wisps unravelled themselves from her legs and she expected to see the peak before her eyes – there was nothing to be seen but a curving stretch of rocks and gravel.

The mountain was not as heavy under foot as before, besides which it was easier for her to walk because the wind that had been blowing against her back, like a mild breeze at first and later more blustery, had now become a strong current of air driving her onwards. It actually lifted her from below and shoved her across the barren ground.

Eventually she thought that she had reached the top of the mountain at last, although she did not notice any peak there. A hint of vegetation took over and the rough wind stroked stunted plants.

Gradually the weather grew calmer, then it became absolutely still. A disturbing feeling came over her. She felt how tired she was after the wind stopped helping her on her way, but she was not going to sit down. She knew that she was alone, no one had any idea where she had gone, if anything happened to her she would have to look after herself or die, alone and with no one to help her. As she stumbled on, her feet sore from walking, she began to long to see the lake. It must be somewhere, improbable as it was for a lake to be on the top of a mountain. The land was sloping to the south by now; she could clearly tell that she was on the way back down and walked for a long time, but the lake was nowhere to be seen. In her eyes the mountain was endless, with one hill and mound taking over from the next, and it towered so high that it seemed to soar up in the sky. The earth below, on the other side of it, could only be seen vaguely, far away in a heat haze. Somewhere out there in the endless distance is my home, she thought, and tried to focus on the invisible but could see only landscape, mountains and glittering rivers which she did not recognize at all. Everything was so strangely distant from her.

Now she was walking on beds of moss with the odd clump of heather among them, but there were no berries on it. There was nothing alive around her, no birds, no animals. The world was alone, far away, not beautiful and not ugly either. She wanted to throw herself down on to the moss and let herself be crushed by the vastness, but then it occurred to her that she must come across the farmhand somewhere, he would come to her, dead, across the beds of moss, but he didn't. No one came, no matter how she tried to get him to join her on her walk with his diaries and say, 'At last you've come . . .'

There was no sound to be heard, no speech, and then she thought, 'There can't be the same kind of lake on top of all the mountains around here.'

She scanned around and saw that the mountains were of various heights, and she went on thinking, 'It's not true that a secret tunnel lies between them deep down in the earth, joining them up to each other. If there are any lakes on top of them, there must be one each, one per mountain, because lakes are like that too, even the ones in places where people live.'

But then she noticed something ahead of her. She had reached the brow of a small hill and could not only make out the landscape at the foot of the mountain, helped by the way the sun was shining, but also noticed a smooth patch ahead of her with something on it resembling water.

She was seized by terror and froze, but curiosity drove her on down the slope and then there was no mistaking it, it was a fairly big lake, greyish blue and full of some kind of vegetation that resembled seaweed but couldn't be that, so far from the sea and up on the top of a mountain, unless the sea was carried there through tunnels that reached to the ocean.

If I throw myself into the lake I might be sucked down through it and into the tunnel, I'd be a long time on my way to the bowels of the earth, but then I'd bob up to the surface and see . . . that I was back home.

Then she heard a sheep bleating. She looked down at the lake and saw a sheep standing there with its lamb. It was standing out on a kind of headland that was covered with long grass or sedge and projected out into the lake. At first she wanted to go over to the sheep, but the terror held her back. She did not want to risk going near the water.

The sun was shining and it was peaceful in the silence. Never before had she felt so much peace as in this terrible stillness. She was in another world where vegetation reigned supreme, the lake, hardy plants, silence, and then this sheep which had its lamb with it. More to the point the lamb moved closer to its mother, who sniffed it and could tell that the smell was wonderfully good: she owned it.

The girl made her way cautiously down the grassy hillside, her eyes fixed on the sheep to prevent it vanishing like a mirage. She drew closer to the lake. Now she could see the vegetation and calmness better. The lamb stood calmly and safely beside its mother, who bent down towards something in the grass, bumping its horns against it. Then it seemed to be rolling a grey and dirty loose clump of wool in front of it.

What's that? the girl wondered.

Then she heard a terrifying draught. She did not know where the rushing sound came from. It swept across like a heavy storm from all directions. Then she saw a huge shadow above her. And at the same moment a snow-white swan swooped down over the sheep. It happened almost in a flash. The bird somehow spread its wings over the whole world and beat them hard at the same time as it arched its neck and curled in the sky. The wing struck a mighty blow against the sheep, which rolled helplessly on to its side. The lamb tried to run over to it, but then the swan came straight back with thundering wings and struck it so hard that it was dashed far out into the lake. Then the sheep scrambled to its feet and jumped away.

The girl sat down, paralysed by terror, but got up at once. She could see the lamb thrashing around in the water but making no headway. The sheep darted about, but did not bleat. It occurred to the girl to run down to the lake to rescue the lamb, but then she saw how its wool was weighing it down and the plants were twining around it; she could never save it.

The swan had alighted. It lifted its wings high up in an arch and approached what she had taken for a clump of wool, but could now see that it was not, it was probably an unfledged cygnet that belonged to the swan in the sedge there. It kept its wings aloft for a long time and scanned around, not as if afraid and fearing an attack from the sheep, but rather because raised wings were a symbol of triumph: it was the swan that owned the lake.

Now the swan took off again. She threw herself to the ground and could feel the draught above her, and expected the swan to sweep her up into the sky with its mighty wings and fling her out into the lake to the lamb, and she would not be able to swim ashore and save herself, because the plants would wrap around her and she would drown. She closed her eyes. She waited. The beating disappeared, and the calm and absolute stillness returned. Not a sound could be heard. She looked up and saw the sun was shining. The swan was nowhere to be seen. Beneath the mountain the landscape glittered in the clear light of afternoon.

'It's getting towards evening,' she thought, and set off by the same route back. She could almost trace her footprints in the trampled moss. 'I'll head straight on, in the same direction all the time, then I'll make it down.'

And so she went on. It was calm and still around her as before, absolutely calm weather, but then she began to feel a slight breeze. She walked into it, farther, farther, and the breeze got up and turned into a rough wind. Now she could see over the mountain. The countryside was bathed in sunshine, a much clearer light than on the mountain's far side. She was still expecting a shadow to descend upon her, that the swan would plunge down and sweep her off the mountain with its wings. But it was her feet that carried her on. They were tired, but she could make her way on them. Now she could see down to the flat plain, as if looking down into vast watery depths. She saw the grey circle of fog a little below her and headed into it. The wind greeted her, welling up against her like a powerful river. It was trying to throw her over backwards, over the edge of the mountain and straight into the lake, but the slope was downwards, her feet found it and overcame her fatigue. She knew she would reach her destination, however exhausted she might be. For that reason she stretched out an arm. The wind whisked her skirt up. The cold latched itself into her bare body, but she took to the air, she felt herself flying onwards, plunged down into the circle of fog and easily slipped through it. Then she saw everything in an instant: the vast panorama, the house at the foot of the mountain, and the fact that all the horses had gone, except the farmer's daughter's horse. And she saw, too, something she could not understand: she saw the snow-white swan flying ahead of her, apparently showing her the way.

MARE'S NEST

Mare's Nest brings the best in international contemporary fiction to an English-language readership, together with associated non-fiction works. As yet, it has concentrated on the flourishing literature of Iceland, which appears under the Shad Thames imprint. The list includes the three Icelandic Nordic Prize-winning novels.

The poetic tradition in Iceland reaches back over a thousand years. The relatively unchanging language allows the great Sagas to be read and enjoyed by all Icelandic speakers. Contemporary writing in Iceland, while vivid and highly idiosyncratic, is coloured and liberated by this Saga background. Closely observed social nuance can exist comfortably within the most exuberant and inventive magic realism.

Brushstrokes of Blue
The Young Poets of Iceland

Edited with an introduction by
Pál Valsson

112 pp.   £6.95   pbk

'Exciting stuff: eight leading northern lights constellated here'
Simon Armitage

A representative introduction to contemporary poetry in Iceland,
Brushstrokes of Blue is full of surprises, from startling surrealist
juxtapositions and irresistible story-spinning to gentle *aperçus* and
the everyday world turned wild side out.

Sigfús Bjartmarsson
Gyrdir Elíasson
Einar Már Gudmundsson
Elísabet Jökulsdóttir
Bragi Ólafsson
Kristin Ómarsdóttir
Sjón
Linda Vilhjálmsdóttir

in lucid translation by
David McDuff,
Sigurdur A. Magnússon
and Bernard Scudder

Epilogue of the Raindrops

Einar Már Gudmundsson

Translated by Bernard Scudder

160 pp.   £7.95   pbk

'A fascinating and distinctive new voice from an unexpected quarter'
Ian McEwan

Magic realism in Iceland is as old as the Sagas. Described by its
translator as 'about the creatures in Iceland who don't show up
in population surveys', *Epilogue of the Raindrops* recounts the
construction (and deconstruction) of a suburb, the spiritual quest of
a mouth-organ-playing minister, the havoc wreaked by long-drowned
sailors, and an ale-oiled tale told beneath a whale skeleton, while the
rain falls and falls and falls.

Justice Undone

Thor Vilhjálmsson

Translated by Bernard Scudder

Nordic Prize 1988

232 pp.   £8.95   pbk

'Thor Vilhjálmsson's hallucinatory imagination creates an eerily
beautiful vision of things, Icelandic in far-seeing clarity, precision,
strangeness. Unique and unforgettable.'
Ted Hughes

Based on a true story of incest and infanticide and set in the remote
hinterland of nineteenth-century Iceland, *Justice Undone* is a
compelling novel of obsession and aversion. An idealistic young
magistrate (a figure inspired by the Whitmanesque Icelandic writer
Einar Benediktsson) undertakes his first case. His geographical and
emotional journey into bleak, unknown territory, where dream
mingles sensuously with the world of the Sagas, tests him to the limit.

Angels of the Universe

Einar Már Gudmundsson

Translated by Bernard Scudder

Nordic Prize 1995

176 pp.   £7.95   pbk

'I'm one of those invisible citizens that the wind sweeps along . . .
I only make myself known when the volcanoes start rumbling
within my soul.'

With humane and imaginative insight, Gudmundsson charts Paul's
mental disintegration. The novel's tragic undertow is illuminated
by the writer's characteristic humour and the quirkiness of his
exuberant array of characters whose inner worlds are
gloriously at odds with conventional reality.

'Einar Már Gudmundsson, perhaps the most distinguished writer of
his generation, is generally credited with liberating serious writing in
his country from an overawed involvement in its own past, and with
turning for inspiration to the icon-makers of the contemporary world.'
Paul Binding, *The Times Literary Supplement*

Night Watch

Frída Á. Sigurdardóttir

Translated by Katjana Edwardsen

Nordic Prize 1992

176 pp.   £7.95   pbk

'We all dangle from umbilical cords . . .'

Who is Nina? The capable, self-possessed, independent,
advertising executive, the thoroughly modern Reykjavík woman?
Or is she the sum total of the lives of the women of her family,
whose stories of yearning, loss, challenge and chance absorb her
as she watches by the bed of her dying mother?

'She has written a book that has no equal in recent Icelandic
literature. It is remarkably well written and tells several stories
that all merge into one . . .'
Susanna Svavasdóttir, *Morgunbladid*

Trolls' Cathedral

Ólafur Gunnarsson

Translated by David McDuff and Jill Burrows

304 pp.   £8.95   pbk

The architect yearns to create a cathedral echoing the arc of a seabird's wing, the hollows of a cliff-face cave. His struggles with debt and self-doubt appear to be over when a seemingly random act, an assault of his young son, destroys him and his family. Obsessions, dreams and memories lead, inevitably, to violence.

'It is a vagrant, morally unsettled form of story-telling on the same wavelength . . . as Dostoevsky.'
Jasper Rees, *The Times*

'Readers may be reminded of the work of the Japanese writer, Shusaku Endo, a fellow Catholic, who also can combine a scrupulous naturalism with a sense of metaphysical forces at work . . . *Trolls' Cathedral* is a formidable work, mesmerically readable.'
Paul Binding, *The Times Literary Supplement*